P9-CRN-689

CASSIE MILES

UNDERCOVER COLORADO

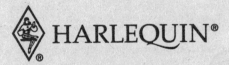

HARLEQUIN®

TORONTO • NEW YORK • LONDON
AMSTERDAM • PARIS • SYDNEY • HAMBURG
STOCKHOLM • ATHENS • TOKYO • MILAN • MADRID
PRAGUE • WARSAW • BUDAPEST • AUCKLAND

To Linda Hull and Jan Gurney,
the powers that be. And, as always, to Rick.

ISBN 0-373-88678-0

UNDERCOVER COLORADO

"According to this cover story, I'm supposed to be falling in love with you. Right?"

"That's the story."

"That might be more believable if it was more true." He rose from the bed and took one step to stand in front of her. "Both times when we kissed, it was a lie."

Her breath caught in her throat. She knew what was coming next.

He took her hands and pulled her to her feet. "Kiss me now, as yourself."

"That might not be wise." Even as she spoke, she knew resistance was futile. With every fiber of her being, she wanted to kiss him.

"Kiss me, Abigail Nelson."

She melted into his arms. When their lips met, it was different than their other kisses. Instead of fierce and demanding, he was oh-so-gentle.

Her arm encircled his torso. Their bodies skimmed against each other. Sensation built gradually, slowly. Oh yes, this kiss was very different.

ABOUT THE AUTHOR

For Cassie Miles, the best part about writing a story set in Eagle County near the Vail ski area is the ready-made excuse to head into the mountains for research. Though the winter snows are great for skiing, her favorite season is fall when the aspens turn gold.

The rest of the time, Cassie lives in Denver where she takes urban hikes around Cheesman Park, reads a ton and critiques often. Her current plans include a Vespa and a road trip, despite eye-rolling objections from her adult children.

Books by Cassie Miles

CAST OF CHARACTERS

Mac Granger—The cynical Denver cop, wounded in the line of duty, becomes part of a bigger sting operation.

Abby Nelson—The FBI Special Agent goes undercover as sex bomb Vanessa Nye to entrap a dirty cop.

Sheila Hartman—Mac's partner is always in the wrong place at the wrong time.

Hal Perkins—Mac's lieutenant at the Denver PD.

Vince Elliot—The vice cop has been on the trail of a drug lord for months.

Nicholas Dirk—The high-powered mogul in Vail is involved in shady dealings.

Leo Fisher—Abby's former fiancé, the FBI undercover agent obsesses about his suspects.

Julia Last—FBI Special Agent in charge of safe house operations.

Roger Flannery—The rookie FBI agent always gets the worst assignments.

Paul Hemmings—Eagle County Deputy Sheriff and Mac's boyhood friend.

Jess Isler—Member of the Vail Ski Patrol and Mac's buddy.

Chapter One

The gun weighed heavy in his hand. The last time Detective Mac Granger unholstered his piece was three months ago at the shooting range when he drilled the heart of the paper target nine out of ten shots.

It was a Thursday night in September. Mac and his partner, Detective Sheila Hartman, had been on their way to a homicide investigation in north Denver when a squawk came over the radio in their unmarked car: "Officer in need of assistance."

Headed north on Park Street, they had just passed the homeless mission with the red neon Jesus Saves sign. They were close to the location given and arrived first on the scene—a dark, deserted city street lined with two- and three-story buildings. The crumbling bricks were stained by years of greasy soot from the nearby railyards.

Three other cars were carelessly parked near a run-down warehouse. The door to the loading dock gaped open. Inside the warehouse, it was pitch-dark.

As Mac emerged from the car, gun in hand, the night breeze whipped around him. A crumpled sheet of newspaper rolled down the street like a tumbleweed. From ten blocks away, he heard a resounding cheer from the baseball fans at Coors Field where the Rockies were playing a night game. Home run.

From inside the warehouse, gunfire exploded. Several shots in rapid succession. A semiautomatic weapon. This sounded like something bigger than he and his partner could handle. "Stay back," he ordered Sheila. "Other patrol cars will be here in a minute."

She shot him a glare. Sheila was inexperienced and willful. She could be a real pain in the ass.

"Police," she yelled. "Throw down your weapons and come out with your hands up."

"Come and get us," was the response.

"Us," Mac said pointedly. "There's more than one."

Ignoring him, Sheila yelled again. "You're surrounded. Give up now."

He cursed under his breath. If the bad guys came onto the street, they could see at a glance that the only cops on the scene were the two of them. Frankly, he and Sheila weren't real impressive when it came to firepower.

"Stay here," he said to her.

"Maybe I could circle around and—"

"Stay."

The woman was impossible. They wouldn't even have been in this area if they'd gone directly to their crime scene in north Denver instead of stopping once because Sheila had to pee, then again because she wanted a latte.

Mac ran toward the loading dock and flattened himself against the brick wall. If anybody came out, they'd be caught between him and his partner.

A bulky figure charged through the open maw of the loading dock and leaped down from the ledge. He landed on the pavement only a few yards away from Mac.

"Drop your weapon," Mac ordered. "Raise your arms."

Immediately, the man obeyed. Mac grabbed his arm and flung him face-first against the brick wall. It was Vince Elliot, an undercover vice cop.

Vince gave no sign of recognition. Even in the heat of confrontation, he didn't break cover.

As Mac cuffed him, he whispered, "This is a drug sting gone bad. Be careful. I want to take these guys alive."

Sheila abandoned her position and came toward them. Dumb move. The worst thing they could do in this situation was to stand together and get mowed down by one blast.

Angrily, Mac motioned for her to go back. He could hear the sirens of approaching patrol cars. Backup was on the way.

Sheila made a confused gesture. Then she stamped her foot and checked her wristwatch as if she were late for a manicure appointment.

Four armed men emerged from the dark warehouse. The one in front aimed directly at Sheila.

Mac had to protect his partner. He fired once, point-blank. The man with the gun went down.

Time froze. Everything went into slow

motion. Mac shoved Vince Elliot to the pavement and stepped in front of him. He looked into the faces of the armed men who turned toward him. He saw panic in their eyes. When they returned fire, he imagined the bullets poised in midair. The thunder of gunshots resounded against brick walls.

It occurred to Mac that he might die right here on this cold city street. A fitting place. Though he had been born and raised in the mountains, this was where he belonged.

He got off another shot, aiming low. He didn't want to kill these guys. Another man fell with a scream.

The others ran toward their car.

"Freeze," Sheila yelled. "Police. Freeze."

The two remaining men dropped their weapons as several patrol cars arrived simultaneously. It was over.

Mac felt a sharp pain in his shoulder and looked down. Blood seeped through his tan sports jacket. He'd been hit.

ABBY NELSON leaned her back against the slender white trunk of an aspen tree and looked up through a canopy of sunlit golden leaves. A fresh wind rustled the boughs, and she glimpsed the clear, blue Colorado sky. Fantastic! This was a truly cherry assignment.

Her last undercover job as an FBI special agent had been in an inner city back east where she was supposed to be a pregnant runaway with a drug habit. Needless to say, her companions were the dregs of society— slimeballs, creeps and heinous criminals, many of whom were going to be locked up for a very long time thanks to Abby's efforts.

But this time? Way better! When she was told that she was going undercover to an FBI safe house in the Colorado Rockies, Abby couldn't believe her luck. She inhaled the crisp clean air and reveled in the spectacular scenery. This was practically a vacation.

Her undercover identity was Vanessa Nye, a protected witness who was waiting to testify at a high-profile case in Los Angeles involving the Santoro crime family. The real Vanessa was an unabashed gold digger who traded on her outrageous sexuality, and Abby had disguised herself accordingly. She dyed her hair platinum blond, heaped on tons of makeup and slithered into skintight clothes. The worst part of her Vanessa outfit had to be these wretched spike heels that were digging holes in the soil beside the aspen trees. She wasn't looking forward to the mile-and-a-half hike back to her bedroom at the safe house.

Her solitude was interrupted when a sturdy-looking woman on horseback rode toward her. Julia Last was the special agent in charge of the FBI safe house known as Last's Resort. She was the only person on site who had been informed that "Vanessa" was a cover for Special Agent Abby Nelson.

Julia gave a friendly wave. "Want a ride?"

"You bet I do."

Julia stared pointedly at the purple high-heeled shoes. "When you get into an undercover role, you don't kid around. How do you stand in those things?"

"Not very well," Abby admitted. "It's not something they teach at Quantico."

Julia flicked the reins and directed her dappled gray mare close to a granite ledge. "Climb on the rocks, then throw your leg over the rear behind the saddle."

Abby moved carefully. Her snug designer slacks were partly spandex, but she didn't want to take a chance on stretching them out and ruining her look. "If I were the real Vanessa, I'd never do this."

"If you were the real Vanessa, I wouldn't have let you wander off by yourself." As soon as Abby was settled, Julia nudged her horse into a steady, rolling walk. "We take security for our protected witnesses very seriously."

"Have you had problems?"

"Not from outside," Julia said. "Our location is remote enough to provide natural protection. As far as anybody knows, this safe house is just another mountain resort. The problems come when witnesses get bored."

"Cabin fever. They want to take side trips to Vail, right? Or invite a friend to visit."

"That's right." When Julia nodded, her curly brown ponytail bounced. "Sometimes we indulge them with supervised outings."

"And you've only got the other two agents working with you?"

"On a rotating basis. This safe house is considered a prime assignment until they get here and find out that their responsibilities include chopping wood, mucking out the stalls for the horses and making beds." She tossed a grin over her shoulder. "I take a certain amount of satisfaction seeing these macho agents doing housework."

"I'll try not to gloat when I see them with feather dusters. What's the name of the young one?"

"Roger Flannery. Nice kid."

Abby tucked a wisp of platinum hair behind her ear. "How many other people are staying here?"

"Two," Julia said. "We refer to them as guests. Both older guys. They've been here for nearly a month."

"I thought the protected witnesses got shuffled more frequently so nobody can get a bead on their location."

"I didn't say they were both witnesses."

Abby already knew that the safe house was used for more than protected witnesses. Sometimes, the feds held high-level meetings here. Sometimes, this idyllic mountain setting provided a place for rest and recuperation for injured agents and cops. "The guy I'm interested in will show up this afternoon."

"The homicide detective from Denver."

Mac Granger was Abby's assignment. He was a Denver cop who had been wounded in a drug sting and was suspected of being on the take which—in Abby's opinion—made him the lowest of the low.

According to her information, he'd wounded an undercover FBI agent at the sting—an agent Abby knew very well. Leo Fisher was her former fiancé.

Though their breakup had been exceedingly nasty, she didn't wish Leo dead. At least, not most of the time. She'd been glad to hear that he was expected to recover from the bullet wound in his leg.

As she rocked on the rump of the horse and watched the landscape unfolding around her, a familiar twinge of regret brushed through her. Too bad things hadn't worked out with Leo. For a while, she'd thought she loved him.

But she wasn't sure. Because they were both undercover agents, it was possible they were both playing at being in love—acting the way they thought people in love ought to behave. With all her undercover identities, she sometimes forgot what it meant to be real.

Her thoughts returned to her current assignment. In addition to shooting Leo in the leg, Mac Granger had gunned down and killed a drug dealer who had been watched by the FBI and Denver vice cops for months in an unusual cooperative investigation. Usually, the death of a drug dealer was no cause for mourning, but this particular guy had indicated a willingness to talk about higher-ups in the drug distribution chain *and about dirty cops.* Now he was dead, thanks to Mac Granger. It made sense that Mac had killed the dealer to keep him from talking.

Because Mac was off duty during the obligatory Internal Affairs investigation into the fatal shoot-ing, his lieutenant had agreed with the FBI plan for Mac to go to the FBI safe house—the location of which was, of course, undisclosed except to Mac who was supposed to relax and take time for his wound to heal.

That was where Abby came in. Her job was to befriend Mac Granger and to ultimately offer him a bribe.

Julia glanced over her shoulder. "Is there anything you can tell me about your assignment?"

"I can guarantee that you're going to hate the way I'll be acting around Mac Granger."

"As Vanessa?"

"The high-powered sex-bomb," Abby said. "I want to attract his attention."

"With the way you're dressed, that shouldn't be a problem. Roger started drooling the minute you arrived."

"We won't tell Roger that I have a third-degree black belt in karate."

"Lethal," Julia said. "And I'm glad. If you were the real Vanessa, I'd worry about keeping you in line."

"It's all an act," Abby assured her. Always an act.

At the top of a rise, they looked down at the safe house which was at the end of a graded gravel road. The two-story cedar structure had a large covered porch at the front. On the opposite side was a sundeck that overlooked a barn and two storage sheds.

"I see an unfamiliar car," Julia said.

"Must be Mac."

"That's odd." There was a hint of irritation in her voice. "We usually don't allow our guests to have their own transportation."

Part of the plan was to allow Mac some mobility in the hope that he might implicate himself. "I promise to keep close surveillance on him."

When they entered the safe house, Abby made an immediate detour to her upstairs bedroom. The first thing she did was kick off the spike heels and flex her aching toes. Why would anyone wear these things on purpose?

In the bathroom, she repaired the dramatic makeup that made her brown eyes look huge and dewy. She applied a fresh coat of fire engine-red lipstick. Putting on all this sleazy glamor wasn't nearly as difficult as maintaining a believable attitude for a gold-digging bimbo.

Though she had no intention of seducing Mac Granger, she wanted him to notice her. She plumped up her boobs inside her fuzzy pink sweater. With her feet wedged into the high heels again, she sashayed down the staircase toward the kitchen.

From inside the kitchen, she heard Julia giving Mac the rules of the house.

"You'll need to make your own bed," Julia said. "And keep your room tidy. We aren't a maid service, but we do provide three square meals a day. If you have any special dietary requirements, you need to tell me."

"No problems." The deep male voice sounded cranky. "What else?"

"No weapons. No visitors. Don't leave without notifying me or one of the other agents. And, obviously, tell no one that this is a safe house."

"Fine," he said. "I'm going into Redding tonight. I grew up here and have a couple of buddies who live nearby. We're going to meet at the tavern."

Interesting, Abby thought. From her brief bio of Mac Granger, she knew he was born near here and attended the local high school. But she hadn't been aware that he still had ties in the area.

She slithered into the kitchen and took her first look at Detective Mac Granger. He stood just over six feet tall and was very nicely put together with a broad chest and narrow hips in button-fly Levi's. He wore a loose-fitting, fisherman's knit sweater in the same dark blue as a policeman's uniform. His sandy blond hair was neatly trimmed and combed straight back from his forehead. Though Mac had grown up in the mountains, his blue eyes showed the world-weary expression of an urban homicide cop who had seen too much. It wasn't going to be easy to outsmart him.

Julia introduced them, using first names only, and asked, "Vanessa, would you like to help pre-pare dinner?"

"Cooking?" In her role as the spoiled hussy, Abby gave an appalled gasp. "Oh, honey. I don't cook."

"Never?"

"I barely even eat. But I do mix a great martini." She zeroed in on Mac. "I'm ever so pleased to meet you."

He turned toward Julia. "I'd be glad to help with dinner."

Abby scowled. Mac hadn't shown the least bit of interest, hadn't even glanced at her cleavage which—thanks to a WonderBra—was as significant as the Grand Canyon.

As Julia set Mac to work, slicing fresh veggies for a tossed salad, Abby sidled up beside him. Rub-bing against his arm, she purred, "Let me help you with that."

"Grab a knife," he said as he rolled a cucumber across the countertop toward her.

She picked up the cucumber and caressed it—a hopefully unsubtle innuendo. "Tell me about your-self, Mac. Where are you from?"

"Denver."

"I thought you were from around here."

He shot a suspicious glance in her direction. "Why would you think that?"

"I heard you talking before I came in." She fluttered her fake eyelashes. "Is it true? Are you a mountain man?"

"Not anymore. I left Redding when I was eighteen."

"But I bet you still ski. You look athletic." She squeezed his bicep. "I bet you're real good at sports."

He shrugged off her grasp and concentrated on slicing a tomato. Talk about unresponsive! This disregard had to stop right now. Abby purposely sliced too close to her index finger and nicked it.

"Ow. Ow. Ow," she wailed. "I cut myself."

She held up her finger so Mac could see the drop of fresh blood beside her French tip manicure. In a baby voice, she said, "Would you kiss it and make it better?"

He glared. "That's not going to happen."

At least, he was looking. Maintaining eye contact with him, she placed her cut finger on her tongue, closed her lips around it and sucked.

His eyebrow lifted. Though he said nothing, his expression showed utter disdain. Calmly, he returned to his chopping.

She pulled her finger out of her mouth with a pop and glanced at Julia who was doing her best not to smirk.

Apparently, the sexy vamp act wasn't going to work on Mac. So what kind of woman did he like? Somebody cute who made him laugh? A helpless damsel in distress?

Julia asked, "Want a bandage?"

"I guess I'll be okay." Abby didn't bother with a sexy pout. Mac wasn't looking. "I don't like this cooking. I want to set the table."

After Julia showed her the plates and silverware, Abby carried them to the dining room. She turned a task that should have taken a few minutes into a big production, moving a dried flower display from the great room to the center of the long oak table. Maybe Mac liked the "happy homemaker" type.

When he appeared in the kitchen doorway, she fussed. "These flowers aren't right. You know what would be really beautiful? I saw some golden aspen leaves outside. We should pick some and put them in a vase."

"Great idea," Julia called from the kitchen.

"While you're outside, you can bring in a few more logs for the fireplace."

Abby made one more attempt to get Mac's attention with her sexy disguise. Since he didn't seem impressed by her boobs or her fluttering eyelashes, she figured he might be the kind of guy who liked to look at bottoms.

As she shuffled the dinnerware, she purposely dropped a fork to the floor. Turning strategically, she bent down to pick it up, giving Mac a full view of her rear end in her snug purple slacks.

She peeked over her shoulder. He wasn't paying the least bit of attention. Geez! What did it take to get this guy interested?

Chapter Two

The blonde had "high maintenance" written all over her, and Mac had made the mistake of getting involved with that kind of woman before. Not this time.

Carefully averting his gaze from any of her body parts that jiggled, he followed her outside to the deck behind the safe house. The sun had set, and the afterglow gilded the underbellies of the clouds. A wide valley spread before him. The buffalo grass had faded to dusty brown and the forested hillsides were pocketed with groves of brilliant yellow aspen.

He'd grown up here. This land was his home. And he hated being back. There were too many memories, too many regrets.

"Oh, Mac," Vanessa called. "I need a big, strong man to help me reach these high branches."

What she needed was a muzzle and a sheet to drape over that delectable body. He trod heavily down the steps from the deck, and stood beside her.

"Up here," she said, handing him the snippers Julia had provided. "This is a pretty branch."

When Mac reached up with his left arm, he experienced a throbbing ache in his shoulder. It was only three days since he'd been shot, and the wound wasn't close to being healed. The doctors told him he'd been lucky. No bones had been broken, but ligaments and muscles were stressed. The bullet had lodged against his scapula, requiring a surgical incision to remove it. The scar required twenty stitches.

He'd lost some blood and was still weak. His AC joint was sore, and he wasn't supposed to lift his left arm higher than his shoulder. But he sure as hell wasn't an invalid who needed enforced recuperation time. There was some other reason Lieutenant Hal Perkins had insisted that Mac come to this FBI safe house during the Internal Affairs investigation. But why?

Mac had known something was up when the lieutenant had called him into his office and told him to close the door. Hal Perkins hadn't smiled; he never smiled. His voice sounded like he had a mouthful of rocks. "You're going on vacation. There's a place in the mountains where you're going to spend some time to heal."

"Not necessary," Mac had said.

"You'll like it. The feds arranged it."

"The feds?" That didn't make sense. Denver P.D. seldom even talked to the feds, much less cooperated with them. "Why?"

"You don't need to know." Perkins sank heavily behind his desk and pulled a stack of papers toward him. "You'll be contacted and given directions."

"What if I don't want to go?"

"Then you can consider this a direct order," Perkins growled. "Don't be a jackass, Mac. This is a gift. An all-expenses-paid vacation in the mountains. Accept it, okay?"

"I don't get it. I shot that undercover agent. There's no reason for the feds to give me a gift."

Perkins shrugged. "Maybe they feel bad on account of you got shot at their sting."

"I thought it was our sting. Vince Elliot was on scene."

"Don't start, Mac. Just go to the mountains." He glared. "And I will need your badge until the I.A. investigation is over."

Silently, Mac had pried his shield from his wallet and placed it on the lieutenant's desktop. He'd already turned over his service handgun.

"Okay," Perkins said. "See you next week."

As soon as he left Perkins's office, Mac had gone to vice looking for answers. He'd talked to Vince Elliot. In spite of the fact that Mac had probably saved his life at the warehouse, the vice cop was cold. Vince said that all he wanted was a bust, then he turned and walked away.

Why all the secrecy? Why wouldn't anybody tell him anything?

"Mac," the blonde whined. "Aren't you going to cut the branches for me?"

He clipped two lower branches that he could reach with his right hand.

"What's wrong?" she asked.

He wished he knew the answer to that question.

THREE HOURS LATER, Mac stepped through the door of the Sundown Tavern in Redding. It felt like he'd gone back in time fifteen years. Not much had changed since high school when Mac and his buddies came here to play pool in the back room. The pine paneled walls still held sepia photographs of legendary skiers and other Colorado sports heroes, notably John Elway. The musty smell of old logs and beer was the same. The wood floor still creaked when Mac walked across it. The light was dim except for the neon beer signs over the bar where a couple of old-timers hunched on stools nursing their drinks.

At the end of the bar, Mac spotted his friend, Paul Hemmings. He'd changed. A lot.

No longer the skinny teenager, Paul was six feet, four inches tall and built like a line-backer. For the past seven years, he'd been an Eagle County deputy sheriff. After his divorce, he was raising two little girls on his own; he carried a lot of responsibility on those big shoulders.

He lumbered across the creaky wood floor like a St. Bernard coming to the rescue of a stranded skier. His huge arms enveloped Mac in a hug that caused a poignant ache in his wounded shoulder.

"That's enough," Mac said.

Paul backed away quickly. "I didn't hurt you, did I?"

"I'm fine."

"I can't believe you got shot in the line of duty. You're supposed to be the smart one."

"Not this time."

After a round of hellos to the other men in the bar who remembered Mac or at least pretended they did, they went into the back room where liquor wasn't served. There were a handful of teenagers back here, eating burgers and giggling.

Paul rolled a cue ball across the green felt of one of the pool tables. "Do you feel up to a game?"

"Bring it on," Mac said. "I can still beat you with one hand tied behind my back."

As Paul racked up the balls, he said, "Tell me about the shooting."

"We heard the call for an officer in need of assistance. Me and my partner, Sheila—"

"You have a woman partner? How's that?"

"I like female partners. They're usually smarter than the men and know the rules. It's never been a problem."

Not until Sheila came along. A lot of what happened at the warehouse had been her fault. First, she'd yelled and provoked the bad guys before sufficient backup was in place. Then, she'd gotten herself in the line of fire.

Mac had downplayed her incompetence when he talked to the I.A. investigators; it wasn't right to rat out your partner. But Sheila had made two dumb moves. That was nearly enough to put her in the same classification as that high-maintenance blonde at the safe house.

The thought of Vanessa brought an unexpected grin. All her prancing and posing made an amusing diversion, especially after she gave up on seducing him and dropped the sex-bomb act. During dinner, she'd rattled on about this and that. At one point, she'd given them a hilarious rendition of her act as a Las Vegas showgirl balancing a wineglass on her cleavage. He had a sense that she was more intelligent than she let on. Street smart, anyway.

Mac picked a cue from the wall rack and tested it. "We're playing eight ball. I'll break."

"Fine with me." Paul leaned on his cue. "So how'd you get shot?"

"I'm not proud of what happened." Mac stretched himself across the pool table, testing different positions that wouldn't strain his left arm and shoulder. He zeroed in on the cue ball and fired. The balls scattered across the table. He sank the seven. "I was in the wrong place at the wrong time."

"It happens."

"Tell me about you," Mac said. "How are the girls?"

"Too smart for their own good. Apparently, at age seven and nine, they know everything. And I'm an idiot."

"I could have told them that." Mac sank another ball. "How about sports? Are they skiing?"

"Skating," Paul muttered. "Figure skating with the fancy outfits and the show tunes."

Mac bit the inside of his cheek to keep from laughing at the thought of his big, husky friend shepherding around his two little princesses.

Mac missed his next shot and stepped back from the table in time to see their friend, Jess Isler, stroll through the door. Mac wasn't the only one who noticed. The teenaged girls in the room stopped talking when Jess appeared.

It had been that way all through high

school. Jess was a good-looking man. He was on the ski patrol and lived in nearby Vail.

After enduring another hug, Mac punched Jess on the shoulder. "Are you still dating that movie star?"

"We moved on. It was too much attention. You know, the paparazzi."

"Oh, yeah." Mac rolled his eyes. "Those paparazzi can be a real pain."

Paul stood between them. "It's been a long time since the three of us got together."

"It was your mom's funeral, Mac." Jess shrugged. "Four years ago."

"She was a good woman," Paul said.

Jess nodded.

Mac said nothing. His feelings about his mother were ambivalent. Sure, he had loved her. Kathryn Granger was beautiful and fun, always laughing. But he knew something about Kathryn that nobody else was aware of. She had betrayed the family.

That was one of the reasons he had left town when he graduated high school. It was also one of the reasons he knew never to trust a woman; they would only break your heart.

Speaking of which…he looked up and saw

Vanessa strolling toward the pool table. What the hell was she doing here?

"Hi there," she said in a breathy little voice. "Mac? Aren't you going to introduce me to your friends?"

"This is a private conversation."

Undeterred, she moved toward Paul. When she grasped his huge hand, he had no alternative but to shake. "I'm Vanessa," she said. "And you are?"

"Paul Hemmings." He gave her a sheepish grin. "How do you know Mac?"

"We're both staying at the same little resort."

"I wanted to ask about that place," Paul said. "Why is it called Last's Resort?"

"The woman who runs it is Julia Last," Mac said. Though Paul was his friend and a deputy, he wouldn't betray the true purpose of the safe house. "Nice place. Real quiet. A friend recommended it to me."

"You could have stayed with me," Paul said.

"Or me," Jess put in.

"Thanks, guys." Mac knew his lieutenant had arranged his stay at the safe house for a reason. "But I'm supposed to rest and recuperate. I can't do that with the little girls at your place, Paul. Or with the big girls who are always hanging out with Jess."

Vanessa had picked up a cue. "Whose shot?"

"Mine." Mac stared down at the table. Paul's last shot had left him behind the eight ball. There wasn't much he could do.

"I'll play the winner," Vanessa said.

Though Mac concentrated on their game, he couldn't help listening as Vanessa chatted with handsome Jess. She was the kind of woman who would always focus on the best-looking man in the room. Or the wealthiest. From the platinum blond curls on her head to the toes of her high-heeled boots, she was a gold digger. It annoyed him that her husky laugh tickled pleasantly at the edge of his senses.

"The Vail ski patrol," she said admiringly to Jess. "You must know some famous people."

"Some," he admitted. "Mostly, my job is a great way to get in a lot of skiing. As a bonus, I get to help people."

"Like your friend, the deputy."

"Kind of weird," Jess said. "The three of us were buds in high school, and we all ended up in some kind of law enforcement jobs."

"Ski patrol?" Paul scoffed. "Do you catch a lot of bad guys on the slopes?"

"Tell me about Mac," Vanessa said.

Mac muffed a shot. He didn't want Jess giving her too much information about him. Until he figured out what Vanessa was up to, he didn't want to let his guard down.

"Mac's dad was the sheriff," Jess said. "A good guy. He moved down to Florida after Mac's mom died."

"Does he have other family up here?"

"Aunt Lucille." Jess chuckled.

"Oh, yeah," Paul chimed in. "Good old Aunt Lucille. She's a real character."

Jess picked up where he left off. "The woman has got to be in her seventies, but she still wears flashy clothes and skis like a demon. She competed in the 1952 Winter Olympics when Stein Eriksen won the giant slalom."

"My kind of woman." Vanessa bared her teeth in a grin. "A winner."

"We'll see about that," Paul said. "Looks like you're playing Mac."

As she sashayed toward the pool table, her

dark eyes held a competitive gleam. Mac decided there was no way he'd let her win this game. Unfortunately, when he broke the balls, nothing went in.

When Vanessa positioned herself across the table, he had a spectacular view of her cleavage. Earlier today, her vamping and prancing was a major turnoff. Now, when she wasn't trying to be sexy, he was getting turned on.

With a crisp shot, she sank a striped ball and left herself another good lie.

"Nice," Jess commented.

Gliding around the table, she nudged Mac out of her way. "I don't like losing."

She tapped the cue ball. Another ball tipped into the corner pocket. Now she had a problem. The cue ball was trapped behind two others.

Her eyes narrowed as she considered all the angles. When Vanessa banked the cue and sank the four, it was obvious that she knew what she was doing.

"You're a hustler," Mac said.

"I learned more in Vegas than just shaking my tail feathers."

When her ruby lips spread in a smug grin,

he had the insane urge to kiss the smile off those lips. He didn't want to be attracted to this woman. She was a protected witness. For all he knew, she was up to her pretty brown eyes in danger and disaster—criminal activity of the worst kind.

He only had one more chance to sink a ball. He muffed it. Then she cleared the table and sank the eight.

Grudgingly, he offered approval. "Not bad."

"Beat you."

She tapped her cue against his chest and looked him straight in the eye. What was going on inside her head? He wanted to find out.

Mac was good in a police interrogation when he had the weight of the law on his side. Subtlety wasn't his forte, but he was good at spotting a liar. "Buy you a drink?"

"I'll have a Singapore Sling."

"The Sundown Tavern doesn't do cocktails with umbrellas."

"Then, I'll have the specialty of the house."

As he led the way from the back room to the bar, Mac calculated her body weight and probable resistance to intoxication. It shouldn't take more than three tequila shots to loosen her tongue. Then she'd be ready to tell him anything he wanted to know.

AN HOUR LATER, Abby stared down at the shot glass on the table. It would be her fourth. Though she'd managed to spill more than she drank, she was beginning to feel the effect.

"Drink up," Mac urged. He was sipping soda, claiming that he couldn't mix alcohol with his pain medication. "No need to worry. I'm the designated driver."

She rose to the challenge, lifting her shot glass. "Here's to the mountains."

"To the mountains," echoed Paul and Jess, both of whom were still nursing their first and only glass of beer.

She tossed back the tequila. The fiery liquid burned her tongue, but she held it in her mouth. When she lifted her beer glass to her lips as a chaser, she spit most of the tequila into the glass. Even with all these precautions, she was woozy. Clearly, Mac was trying to get her drunk. But why?

He rested his elbow on the table and

gazed curiously into her eyes. "How are you doing, Vanessa?"

"Great," she said defiantly.

"Feeling a buzz?"

"Nothing I can't handle."

Drunk or not, she could nail his hide to the wall. If he was a dirty cop, she was the woman who could prove it. As she stared back at him, she was momentarily distracted by the devilish spark of amusement in his intense blue eyes. Being with his friends had loosened him up, and he almost seemed to be having fun. When the tension in his face relaxed, it was a very interesting face. Good bone structure. Strong features.

Though he wasn't as gorgeous as Jess and not as likable as Paul, she was intrigued by Mac. He was a man of many secrets. At the same time, he seemed straightforward and solid. Not the kind of guy who broke the rules. Was he dirty?

"You know, Vanessa," he said softly, "from the first time I saw you, you looked familiar. Have we ever met before?"

"Nope," she said.

"It seems like you know me."

At the edge of her alcoholic haze, a

warning bell went off. He was very subtly in-
terrogating her, trying to get her to admit to
a link between them. He suspected her.

Easily, she slid back into her Vanessa
persona. "You and me? Honey, we don't run
in the same circles."

"How can you be so sure?"

"I just am." Though she didn't physically
move away from him, she tried to create
some distance. "And if you're using this as
a pickup line, it's not very good."

"I don't have to pick you up," he pointed
out. "You followed me."

There was no point in pretending she had
come to the Sundown Tavern by coincidence. It had been difficult for Julia to
arrange the logistics for this trip while still
keeping the other safe house agents in the
dark about Abby's true identity. Though
Abby didn't see the agent who had acted as
her chauffeur, she knew he was nearby.

"I didn't come here because of you," she
said. "I just wanted some fun."

"But you're interested in me," he said.

"What an ego!"

Across the table, Jess and Paul seemed to
be observing their interaction with approval.

"When a woman follows a man into town," Mac said, "there's usually a reason."

"What do you know about women?"

She heard snickers from Jess and Paul, but Mac didn't crack a smile. "I know this," he said. "Women are good at manipulating. They have these secret agendas. Clever little plans. What's yours, Vanessa?"

"You know, there's a word for that attitude. Men who don't like women. Misogynist."

"Big word."

She tossed her platinum curls. "Just because a girl is pretty doesn't mean she's dumb."

"Ouch," Jess said. "Score another point for Vanessa."

"Thanks." When she stood, her knees were a bit rubbery. "I need to visit the little girls' room."

She'd made this trip before they'd started drink-ing, and Abby wished she'd left a trail of bread crumbs to lead her back to the rest-rooms. The route led past the bar and a small dining area, which was empty, into a hallway. By the time she got to the door marked Gals, she was walking steadily.

But her head was spinning. Mac seemed to sus-pect her of ulterior motives. Somehow, he'd seen through her cover story. A smart man. And attractive. She was dangerously close to wanting more from him than information.

She had to stop thinking that way. She was a professional and had worked hard to climb through the ranks in the FBI. Mac was her target. There could never be anything between them.

When she placed her hand on the restroom door, she felt someone clutch her shoulder. Acting on instinct, she whirled in her high-heeled boots to break his hold. At the verge of a karate chop, she checked herself. She knew this man. "Leo."

"I like the hair. You make a sexy blonde."

When he reached up to touch her curls, she slapped his hand away. Leo Fisher was no longer her fiancé; he had no right to touch her. "I thought you were in the hospital."

He gestured with a carved ebony cane. "No broken bones. I need some ligament repair on my knee, but it'll wait."

"My sympathies," she said coolly.

His voice lowered. "How long has it been, Abby?"

"Fourth of July. Last year." The moment

when she broke up with him was still vivid in her memory. There was no way she'd ever forgive him. "Tell me why you're here. And make it fast. I need to get back to the table."

"I wanted to keep an eye on your boy, Mac Granger. If he's one of the dirty cops, he might contact the guy I've been looking for."

"This is my assignment."

"I've been working this case for six months, and I'm close to getting enough evidence on the man at the top of the drug distribution chain. He owns a place in Vail. If your friend, Mac, tries to get in touch, let me know."

"Forget it," she said.

"Come on. For old times' sake?"

He was almost pleading, and that worried her more than if he'd come on strong. "Are you supposed to be on this investigation? Does anybody know what you're doing?"

"I'm undercover. You know how it gets."

"Yes, I do." She worried that Leo had come unhinged and was acting on his own as a rogue agent. "I suggest you go back to Denver and get that operation on your knee. Take some time off. Schedule a visit with a counselor."

He handed her a scrap of paper with a phone number written on it. "Call me on my cell phone if Mac Granger goes to Vail."

She crumpled the paper and threw it on the hardwood floor. Then, she turned away from him. "Finding your drug lord isn't my problem."

Her assignment was Mac.

Chapter Three

In a shabby little diner in Denver, three people hunched around a small circular table. Though it was late and nobody was seated nearby, they spoke in low, secretive tones. The topic of their conversation was Mac Granger.

"If he figures this out, he could screw up everything."

"Forget about him. He's stuck in the mountains."

"My point exactly." The speaker took a long drag on a Marlboro Light. "He's close to Vail. If he gets suspicious, he could start making connections."

Nervous tension wrapped around them like a gloved hand. For the moment, they were safe and warm. At any moment, the hand could open, and they'd be exposed.

"Well, what do you think we should do about Mac? Kill him?" A strangled laugh underlined the absurdity of that idea. "We're not murderers."

But the thought had been planted. To kill Mac Granger was the simplest solution. *Better him than us.*

"I don't know him," the smoker said. "You both do. Is he the kind of guy who gives up easily?"

"Never."

"Then he should be eliminated. I'll take care of it."

The other two stared down at their coffee mugs, unwilling to acknowledge the decision, but knowing they had no other choice. Having Mac alive and probably investigating was dangerous.

"Make it look like an accident. I don't want an investigation."

"Don't worry." The cigarette stubbed out in the ashtray, leaving a wisp of smoke. "I'm a cop. I know better than to leave clues."

THE NEXT MORNING, Mac stood on the deck behind the safe house finishing his second mug of coffee. A crisp breeze stirred the dry grasses of the valley and quaked in the golden aspen leaves. The clear blue skies offered the fresh promise of a brand-new day. A new start. He should have felt optimistic.

Instead, a series of dark questions played across his mind. Why had he been sent to this safe house to recuperate? Why wouldn't Vince Elliot, the undercover cop who had been at the warehouse shooting, talk to him? Was Mac under suspicion? Of what?

Last night, he'd called his partner, Sheila, on her cell phone. Though Sheila had all the perceptiveness of a goldfish, she was his partner. She owed him. And she was a good source for gossip. If all her bragging was true, she'd slept with half the Denver P.D. which was probably how she'd gotten promoted to detective so quickly. Without betraying the location of the safe house, Mac had arranged to meet her later today near Redding.

His frustration level rose. He hadn't done anything wrong. He was a good cop. His actions at the warehouse were unfortunate but appropriate. Why the hell would he come under suspicion?

He looked to the mountains for solace. When he was younger, he had loved this land. He and Paul and Jess had taken a blood oath to always stay together in the Rockies. When they were kids, they'd called themselves the Three Trolls, Keepers of the Treasure, and they had ceremoniously buried a shoebox filled with crystal, pyrite and pine cones.

Paul and Jess had lived up to that boyhood oath. Both of them were still here—flourishing and happy.

But not Mac. His vision of life was different. He preferred the in-your-face threat of city life where the scene was constantly evolving and there was a reassuring undercurrent of static noise. All this fresh mountain air was choking him. Last night in bed, he couldn't sleep; the mountain silence weighed down on him.

After less than twenty-four hours here, he was itching to get back to Denver, back to work. The only thing keeping him here was his suspicion of Vanessa. As soon as he understood what she was doing, everything else would become clear.

He returned to the kitchen where Julia had

finished washing the breakfast dishes. Everyone had eaten, except for Vanessa, who hadn't yet made her appearance. He stood in the kitchen doorway and glanced past the dining room table toward the staircase. Where was she?

He asked Julia, "How long has Vanessa been at the safe house?"

"Only a few hours longer than you."

"She's a handful."

"So are you," Julia said with a hint of accusation. "In the future, I'd prefer that you didn't roll into town and get blitzed. This isn't a frat house, Mac."

"I wasn't drinking."

"But Vanessa was. I had a full report from Roger Flannery."

"The young guy?" Mac had met Roger Flannery yesterday. He was so new to his job as an FBI agent that he still had the stink of Quantico about him.

"It was good experience for him to keep surveillance last night," Julia said. "But I don't want it to happen again."

"Yes, ma'am."

There was a loud groan from the staircase, and Mac turned to see Vanessa lurch onto the bottom stair. Her skintight leather pants creaked as she wobbled across the floor toward the kitchen. Her blond hair was a fluffy contrast to her pained expression. In spite of her heavy makeup, he saw dark circles under her big, brown eyes.

"Hangover?" he asked brightly.

As she tried to focus on him, her left eyelid twitched. "Aspirin," she rasped.

"I'd have thought a pool hustler like you could hold her—"

"Aspirin," she interrupted more loudly. "Percoset. Morphine."

Julia took her firmly by the arm and pulled her toward the kitchen. "Come with me, Vanessa. I have a no-fail remedy for hangovers."

"Slow down," Vanessa said. This morning, she seemed incapable of balancing in her high-heeled sandals.

"It'd serve you right to fall flat on your nose," Julia said. "You ought to know better than to drink tequila."

Vanessa came to a halt. She kicked off the high heels. Bare-footed, she plodded into the kitchen.

Though she was teetering at the edge of

misery, Mac could tell that she was still in control, which seemed to be her most pronounced character trait. Control. Even though she'd gotten pretty well oiled at the Sundown Tavern, she wasn't drunk enough to give him any useful information.

Mac had investigated on his own. Last night, after talking to Sheila, he'd contacted a cop buddy in L.A. and asked about a state's witness named Vanessa.

Her full name was Vanessa Lenore Nye. She was a former Vegas showgirl who had lived with the elderly head of the Santoro crime family before turning state's evidence. Mac's first impression of her was one hundred percent correct. She was a woman who'd do anything for the right price. Her extravagance was renowned. Reputedly, she owned half a dozen mink coats and over a hundred pairs of shoes. At one time, she'd been in possession of the famed thirty-four carat LeSalle diamond. *Anything for the right price.*

So why was she interested in him? It was out of character for a gold digger to flirt with a Denver homicide cop who drove a late-model car and didn't wear a Rolex.

In the kitchen, Julia dumped tomato juice,

raw eggs and a nasty-looking green weed into the blender. When she set the dial to puree and turned on the blender, Vanessa winced at the grinding whir.

"Sounds like a 747," she muttered.

"After this remedy," Julia said, "you'll be better in no time."

"Want coffee," Vanessa said pathetically.

"Drink this first." She held out a glass filled to the brim with a putrid green liquid. "Every drop."

Like a swimmer preparing for the hundred meter breaststroke, Vanessa inhaled and exhaled deeply. She took the glass and chugged until it was empty. "Yech."

"Go to the dining room," Julia said. "I'll bring you coffee and dry toast."

At the table, Mac held her chair and took his place at the end of the table beside her. Right now, she appeared to be vulnerable; this might be a good time to start with his probing. "You lived in Los Angeles," he said. "What part of the city?"

"Newport."

That fit with the information he'd been given. "Right near the ocean. Did you have a private beach?"

She held up her hand. "No more talking."

"Ever go surfing?"

Slowly, she turned her head and glared with such cold hostility that she might have been measuring him for a coffin. "No. More. Talk."

He waited until she'd finished her coffee, a glass of water and a piece of toast. Her eyes were more alert.

"Surfing," she said, "is not my thing. Even in a wetsuit, the water is too cold. I like indoor sports."

"So, I assume you're not a skier."

"Love the ski clothes. There just aren't enough times when I can wear my minks."

Julia popped her head around the corner. "Feeling better, Vanessa?"

"A lot better. What did you put in that drink?"

"It's a secret formula. And it always works," Julia said. "The next thing you should do is go for a walk outdoors in the fresh air."

"Good idea," Mac said. "I'll come with you."

THOUGH ABBY would rather have stayed in bed all day, nursing her hangover and cursing the wormy evils of tequila, she didn't have that luxury. Last night, she had recognized Mac's restlessness. He didn't want to be here. And there was no way to force him to stay at the safe house. He had come here at the suggestion of his lieutenant. If he decided to leave, he could do so.

To fulfill her assignment, she needed to convince him to trust her, offer him a bribe and inform her superiors of his response. A hike along a secluded mountain path seemed like a good way to get close to him.

She abandoned her high heels for a pair of bright pink sneakers that matched her low-cut sweater. Together, she and Mac set out on a path that led past the barn toward a sloping hillside. The morning sun beat down with aching clarity. Behind her huge, extra-dark sunglasses, Abby winced. "Is it always so glaring?"

"Take a deep gulp of that fresh air," he said cheerfully. The man was positively enjoying her misery. What a rat! If she hadn't been undercover, Abby would have flattened him with a karate kick to the jaw.

He leaned against the corral beside the barn where three horses pranced and flicked their long tails. "Maybe," he said, "we should go for a ride."

Bouncing up and down in the saddle with her brain crashing inside her skull? "Forget it."

"Look around you. Take a minute to appreciate the scenery."

"If it's so great, how come you live in the city?"

He shrugged. "I just ended up there."

She didn't believe that for one minute. Mac was the kind of man who took action. Things didn't "just happen" to him. "What made you leave?"

"The usual reasons," he said cryptically. "How about you? Did you grow up in Los Angeles or move there?"

Abby couldn't remember if she'd mentioned L.A. last night when she was drinking. After she'd bumped into Leo outside the ladies' room, things had gotten real blurry. She'd felt like she was in a waking dream, standing outside her body and watching herself as she slurped down tequila and laughed too loud. Only her years of undercover experience had kept her from completely blowing her identity as Vanessa Nye.

Now, she knew, Mac was trying to pierce that cover. He must have gotten some inside information about Vanessa Nye and was testing her. Well, fine! Even with the remnants of a hangover, she could handle this.

"I grew up in a little town in Oregon. I didn't hate it, but I was bored. So totally bored. Vegas was more to my liking."

"I like Oregon," Mac said. "What was the name of the town?"

"Sterling." She remembered more details from her dossier on Vanessa. "Our high school team was the Sterling Pirates. Our colors were red and gold. I was a cheerleader."

"And in Las Vegas?"

"Different kind of cheers." She started walking along the path. Vanessa's early life wasn't all that different from her own. Abby had also come from a small town and had been a cheerleader.

"Tell me how you ended up in California."

Abby lowered her sunglasses and peered over the rim at him. "I'm not in the mood for a cat-and-mouse game, Mac. If there's something you want to know from me, just ask."

"You're Vanessa Nye," he said.

"Bingo."

"You lived with the head of the Santoro family."

"Right again."

"Why?"

She allowed her sunglasses to fall back onto the bridge of her nose. How would the real Vanessa handle this inquiry? "None of your business."

Turning away, she tromped along the path beside a narrow creek. The dried grasses at the side of the rippling water crackled as she walked through them. Under her sweater and leather pants, Abby perspired although the temperature was pleasantly cool. She welcomed the cold sweat, evidence that the alcohol was working through her system.

As she followed the creek into the shadow of the trees, she paused. Her goal was to get Mac to trust her, which meant she needed to be more amenable. She forced herself to smile at him. "I don't want to think about the past, okay? I just want to have fun. Just to, you know, be friends with you."

"Maybe I want to be more than a friend."

She hadn't expected that response. All the indications Mac had given until now were that he didn't even know she was female. What was he up to? She studied his expression.

Like all good liars, Abby was easily able to recognize deception in others. It seemed to her that Mac was telling the truth about wanting to hook up with her. His teeth bared in a predatory grin. His gaze latched on to her face, and he leaned close. These were all indications of physical attraction.

Surely not. Surely, she was reading the signs wrong. "What are you saying?"

"I like you."

"Even though you know who I am?" His readiness to get friendly with Vanessa was clearly inappropriate. "But you're a cop."

"So what?"

A good cop would have better boundaries. "Don't you disapprove of my connection with Santoro?"

"That was the past," he said. "I thought you just wanted to have fun."

"Well, sure. But—"

"You could have fun with me." His right arm encircled her waist and he pulled her tight against his hard, lean body. "What do you say, Vanessa?"

Expertly, she slipped away from his one-armed embrace. Too much was happening too fast. Though her brain was still sluggish from the hangover, her instincts warned her about getting close to this man. He was her target.

And she was Vanessa Nye. A gold digger. That would be her excuse to back off. "Well, Mac. If you really know so much about me, you'll know that I'm very selective. My companionship doesn't come cheap."

"You like pretty things," he said.

"Expensive things."

"Today is your lucky day," he said coolly. "I can afford you, Vanessa. I'm rich."

From bribes? From ill-gotten gains? "No way. Cops don't make big bucks."

"Inheritance," he said. "I received a ton of money when my grandmother sold off family-owned lands where Vail ski resort was developed in the 1960s. The Grangers are very, very wealthy."

His gaze flicked down and to the left. His right hand touched the side of his nose and rubbed across his lips. Both were obvious signals that Mac was telling a lie. Abby knew it. *But Vanessa wouldn't.* Vanessa would take Mac at his word.

"Really?" she asked. "You're a land baron?"

"A former land baron. That's right."

He looked down at his toes and shuffled. Clearly uncomfortable. Mac was the worst liar she had ever encountered. He wouldn't last a minute in undercover work.

But this lie—no matter how poorly executed—was very clever as a test. If she really was Vanessa Nye, she'd be all over this good-looking cop who was also rich. Vanessa used seduction to get what she wanted. And, for the moment, Abby was Vanessa.

She purred, "I think you're right, Mac. You and me? We could have some fun together. Later today, you could take me shopping at the boutiques in Vail."

"I don't want to wait until later."

Again, he dragged her into an embrace.

As Vanessa, she wouldn't resist. Abby set aside her own feelings of distaste and played her undercover role as the sexy vamp. Her lips met his. In the back of her mind, she was detached, repeating a mantra. *This is only a job, only a job, only...*

His mouth was fierce and demanding. His arms held her in a viselike grip. Her breasts crushed against his chest.

But when he leaned away from her, she saw a look of surprise in his honest blue eyes. He removed her sunglasses, taking down a barrier between them. She liked what she saw. A strong man.

Though the planes of his face had been hardened by experience, she saw empathy in his eyes—the true kindness that came from understanding. A good man.

Dappled sunlight filtered through the overhanging branches of conifers. The whisper of the creek trickled at the edge of her senses. His arms felt warm and sheltering. It felt right to be with him.

When he kissed her again, her body responded to him. Her well-developed defense system came crashing down as she allowed herself to enjoy the breathtaking sensation of their kiss. Her heart fluttered, and a thrill chased through her entire body.

Oh, God, no. This was all wrong! Mac Granger could be a dirty cop, the worst kind of traitor. She couldn't be attracted to him.

Gasping, she broke away. "That's enough."

They stood, staring at each other.

She saw something in him that touched her soul. He'd been hurt, badly hurt. But he was tough; he could take the pain and come back stronger. Without words, she saw all these things.

She wanted to know him better. To hear his truth.

And she wanted to share her feelings with him, to tell him how tired she was of constantly pretending to be someone else. On the tip of her tongue was her name. Abigail Marie Nelson. She longed to tell him. To be completely, utterly honest.

For the first time in her career as an FBI special agent, Abby had completely forgotten her cover story.

Chapter Four

Mac's plan to unmask the woman who called herself Vanessa Nye went up in smoke when she kissed him back. Until then, he'd been trying to interrogate her, trying to trip her up. When he had demanded a kiss, he figured she'd back off and admit that she was conning him.

He hadn't expected a lightning bolt.

He needed distance from her. And time to sort out his feelings. He spent the rest of the morning avoiding Vanessa and took off early for the meeting he'd scheduled with his partner.

Mac parked outside the graveyard near Redding. A secluded spot at the end of a graded gravel road, this was the first place that had occurred to him when he arranged this meet with Sheila. Mac wanted privacy, and nobody came here by accident. Not that the old cemetery was ominous. The opposite was true. This gently rising hillside surrounded by Ponderosa and lodgepole pine provided a peaceful resting place. The graves—some of them dating back over a hundred years—were fenced off, but the land wasn't manicured. Weeds and wildflowers grew rampant between the simple markers.

As soon as he stepped out of his car, Sheila pulled up beside him in her own vehicle. Good timing. In spite of her many other faults, his partner was punctual.

"Did you take the day off?" he asked as she came toward him.

"That's right." As always, she sounded irritated. "Until you get back, I'm stuck with boring desk work, which I totally hate. If I wanted to spend the entire day hanging around the station, I would have become a lawyer."

He didn't point out that a law degree was probably far beyond her limited ability to concentrate. "Did you get the information I asked for?"

"This time," she said, "you really messed up."

He messed up? He bit down hard to keep

from spitting out accusations. The only mistake he'd made at the warehouse shooting was allowing her to get out of the car. "Tell me what you've heard."

"You don't have any idea how much trouble you're in." Her scowl etched deep lines below her thick brown bangs. "How much do you know about that guy you shot and killed?"

Mac had made it his business to find out about the man whose life he had taken. "His name was Dante Williams, and he was twenty-seven years old. High school dropout. Seven arrests, mostly on drug-related charges. One conviction landed him in prison for eight months."

"A regular poster boy for how to ruin your life."

"He still didn't deserve to die." Though Mac had fired in the line of duty, he would always regret the shooting, and he would visit the grave of Dante Williams to pay his respects. It was a ritual Mac followed with the other victim he'd shot and killed early in his police career.

"Anyway," Sheila said, "this guy, Dante, was about to give evidence on the number one drug distributor in Colorado. The top man. The honcho. When you killed him, you blew it."

"Were the feds and Denver vice working together on the sting?"

"Not on purpose," she said. "They were both following trails that led to the same place."

"To Dante," he said.

"It gets worse." She glanced at her wrist-watch—one of her less annoying nervous habits. "Some people think you killed Dante on purpose. To keep him from turning snitch."

The implication was clear. The FBI and the Denver P.D. suspected that Mac was a dirty cop, that he'd killed Dante Williams on orders from some honcho drug kingpin.

A burst of anger flared behind his eyelids. The shooting at the warehouse had been a grotesque miracle of bad timing, but he shouldn't be a suspect. His dedication to his work and his years of service ought to count for something. He'd earned medals and ci-tations. He was a good cop.

"Now you know," Sheila said with a smirk. Her attitude was smug and superior. She almost seemed to be enjoying his fall from grace. "The best thing for you to do is lay low and let the dust settle. Please, Mac. Will you do that?"

"Why do you care?" His relationship with Sheila had never been good. They bickered like an old married couple at the verge of divorce.

"You're my partner." Insincerity dripped from her voice. "You've got to forget about this. Don't rock the boat. Don't start investigating on your own."

As if he'd take advice from her? If she'd behaved in a competent manner at the warehouse sting, he wouldn't be in this position. Unfortunately, she was his only source of information since everybody else suspected him. He needed to maintain this contact with Sheila. "Did you get that photograph I asked for?"

"Of course." She opened her car door and leaned inside to retrieve a manila envelope. "This is a recent photo of the FBI undercover agent you shot. Leo Fisher. He's out of the hospital."

Mac pulled the photo out of the envelope and studied it. Leo Fisher was an average-looking guy with dark eyes and a square jaw.

His long hair was pulled back in a ponytail. Mac thought he'd spotted Leo Fisher last night at the tavern, but he wasn't one hundred percent sure.

Once again, he tapped into Sheila's vast collection of gossip. "What have you heard about Leo Fisher?"

"He's off the case, but..." Her voice trailed off.

"Come on, Sheila. What have you heard?"

"I heard that Fisher was up here in the mountains. Going to Vail, I think."

"Why?" he asked. Vanessa had also hinted about a trip to Vail.

"I don't know. God, Mac. I can't tell you everything."

Her tone was as whiny as a teenager. He really disliked this woman. Incompetent. Immature.

"I'm thirsty," she said. "Come with me to get a latte."

"Can't," Mac said. He didn't want to spend any more time with her than absolutely necessary.

"Where are you staying up here, anyway?"

"I grew up here. In Redding." No way would

he tell Sheila about the safe house. "I have friends up here."

"Like that cute guy." She was suddenly alert. "I remember him. He stopped by the station to visit you a couple of times, right? He's on the Vail ski patrol. I'd love to see him again."

"Not today."

"At least come with me for coffee. I drove all the way up here. What are you doing that's so important?"

He pushed open the wrought iron gate leading into the cemetery. "Visiting my mother's grave."

Not even Sheila could be argue with the finality of that statement. She backed toward her car. "Bye, Mac. I'll stay in touch."

"You do that," he muttered.

The information she'd given him hadn't been completely unexpected. He'd felt the suspicions. Now, he knew why.

In the cemetery, he picked his way along a hard earth path lined with stones to a section where all the Grangers were buried. His grandparents. His great-uncle. And his mother, Kathryn Granger.

Leaning down, he plucked a few weeds

that obscured the pink marble marker inscribed with her name. He read the words: Beloved Wife and Mother.

It was true. He had loved her. His name—MacCloud—had been her maiden name, and she'd done as well as she could raising him.

But he couldn't respect Kathryn Granger. Not after he saw his mother in the arms of a man who wasn't his father. She'd had an affair. She'd betrayed him and his father, the sheriff. Even after her death, he found it hard to forgive her lies.

Mac doubted he would ever find a woman he could trust.

LEO FISHER limped along the cracked sidewalk on a dark Denver street, not far from the warehouse where he'd been shot in the leg. This was a cruddy part of town, deserted after dark except for the bums and the rats that scattered in fear at his approach.

Leo was alone. Always alone. But he wasn't bitter. He had a job to do, an important job. And he was the only one who could do it right. By himself. Alone.

Seeing Abby had been weird. He'd barely thought about her since the night she walked out on him. Maybe he'd been hard on her, but she should have understood that he was still in character, still playing the undercover role. The hell with her! He didn't want or need a wife and family.

He was the best damned undercover agent in the FBI. The best. And there was no way in hell he'd give up on this operation. Not now when he was so close. Why should he let some snot-nosed vice cop like Vince Elliot step in and grab all the glory? This was Leo's bust.

He stopped on the corner under a street-lamp and lit up a smoke.

A dark form materialized beside him. A snitch.

"Sorry about Dante," Leo said.

The snitch made the sign of the cross. "He was a good man."

"What have you got for me?"

"A name."

Leo scoffed. "I know the name. Nicholas Dirk."

He was the head honcho in drug distribution throughout the Rocky Mountain west. A wealthy guy who dabbled in all kinds of crime under the cover of being a land developer. He had houses in Denver and in Vail.

"I got evidence," the snitch said.

"Give."

"It's on a computer. Dirk always takes the laptop computer with him. Download that and you've got him."

Leo wasn't impressed by this overly obvious information. "Big deal. There's no way for me to get my hands on that evidence."

"For the right price, I can tell you the password."

"Now you're talking." Leo tossed down his cigarette and crushed it with the tip of his cane. That password was worth paying for.

ON THE SECOND FLOOR in the safe house were six bedrooms of varying sizes. Abby's was small and squarish, plain but clean, without a telephone, computer hookup or television. Her bedroom opened into a bathroom that she shared with Mac.

For the past ten minutes, she had been standing with her ear to the bathroom door, listening to the thrum of the shower and debating with herself about opening the door a crack to spy on him.

Obviously, she'd be invading his privacy

big-time. But her job as an undercover agent was to get close to him, and he couldn't ignore her if she walked into the bathroom while he was half-naked. Kind of a risky maneuver. But she had to make him talk to her. She had questions. A lot of questions.

This afternoon, she and Julia had followed him to the cemetery. Abby's surveillance technique was simple. Earlier today, she'd planted a tracking device in the heel of Mac's boot. All she'd needed to do was activate the device. Julia drove and, together, they'd used GPS technology to locate the signal.

From a hillside near the graveyard, they'd watched while Mac met with his partner, Sheila Hartman. Though Abby hadn't been close enough to hear what they were saying, the very fact that he'd arranged a clandestine meet was suspicious. Were they both dirty cops? What kind of plans were they making?

Using binoculars, Abby had seen them exchange a photograph of Leo. Again, suspicious.

Leo had said that he was tracking a drug kingpin who had a home in Vail. Would Mac make contact with this person? Would he demand a payoff for the murder of Dante Williams? Was he on the take?

Abby really hoped not. After that over-whelming kiss this afternoon, she wanted nothing more than to discover that Mac was squeaky clean and above suspicion.

After the noise from his shower ended, she waited a few minutes so he'd have time to put on some clothes. Then she opened the bathroom door a crack and peeked inside.

Her intention was to march right in. Brazen and bold. But the sight of him stopped her.

Wearing only a towel around his waist, Mac stood in front of the sink. His skin was ruddy from the heat of the shower. His back was broad and nicely muscled across his shoulder blades. His torso was lean.

He wasn't perfect, but close. Abby's heart beat in triple time. Her breath caught in her throat. She wanted to forget about this inves-tigation, to burst through this door, to grab a towel and dab the clinging droplets of moisture from his skin. That touch would lead to more. She'd rake her fingers through his crisp chest hair and absorb the warmth from his flesh.

He stared into the mirror, examining the angry red scar on his shoulder. The threads of his stitches were visible. Carefully, he applied an antiseptic salve and stuck on a white rectangular bandage. Then he reached into a leather case and took out an amber prescription bottle. He tapped out two capsules and tossed them down his throat.

Though these were probably pain pills for his injury, she considered the possibility that he might have a drug habit. Addiction had been the undoing of many good men. If Mac was guilty, it was her job to expose him.

She silently cringed. While he was standing in front of her, nearly naked, "expose" might not be the best thought to have floating inside her head.

He turned to face the bathroom door where she was hiding. "Enjoying the view?"

If Abby had been acting like herself, she'd be humiliated beyond belief. But she was Vanessa, the professional slut. In that persona, she pushed the door open wide and leaned against the jamb. Slowly, she exhaled the breath she'd been holding and licked her lips. "Yummy."

"You were spying on me."

"Not really." Abby didn't have to fake the husky tone in her voice; she actually was turned on. "I was going to use the bathroom. It's just a coincidence that you were in here first."

"Most people would say 'excuse me' and close the door."

"I'm not most people." She kept her distance but pointed to the bandage on his arm. "How did you hurt yourself?"

"It's a long story."

"Tell." Most guys would welcome the opportunity to brag about being in a shoot-out at a dark warehouse. She encouraged him to talk. "Were you in danger? Were you very brave?"

"Do you like dangerous men?"

"Of course." Actually, Abby felt quite the opposite. She'd come in contact with enough supposedly dangerous men to know that most of them were macho jerks. "All women love a bad boy."

"Have you ever been in danger?"

"Sure." That wasn't a lie. In her work, Abby frequently came under threat.

"Did you like it?" Mac asked.

She didn't. If she was in danger, it meant she'd made a mistake. Though Vanessa Nye probably wouldn't have the same reaction, it was too late to frame a lie. Abby knew that her honest reaction had already betrayed itself in her expression. Truthfully, she said, "I don't like violence."

Mac's left eyebrow lifted as he assessed her words. His sandy hair—usually combed straight back—fell rakishly across his forehead. "That might be one of the most honest things I've heard you say."

Which meant she wasn't doing a very good job at her cover story. Lying to him was a lot harder than it ought to be, probably due to the fact that he was wearing nothing but a towel that slipped lower on his narrow hips. Abby couldn't remember a time when she'd been so distracted by a scrap of terry cloth.

Again, the truth bubbled out of her. "I want to be honest with you." She should stop right there, but she couldn't. "I want to tell you everything. It feels like I've been hiding behind disguises all my life. I'm always pretending to be something I'm not."

His blue eyes compelled her attention. Beautiful eyes. Honest eyes. It was hard to imagine those eyes could belong to a dirty cop. "Who are you?" he asked.

She wanted so much to tell him, to forget about her assignment and drop her cover. "You know who I am, Mac."

"What do you want from me?"

The truth. As she eased away from the doorway and came a dangerous step closer to him, she resumed her Vanessa persona. "I want to know you better, and I want you to know me. We might be able to help each other."

"How so?"

A shadow of suspicion darkened his expression, and she knew it was too soon to offer the bribe. She needed to gain his trust, to make him her partner. Reaching up, she glided her manicured fingernails along his arm. "I scratch your back. And you scratch mine."

He caught hold of her wrist. His grasp was firm, and the physical contact reminded her that they were only a few steps away from her bed. If he kissed her again, she wasn't sure that she'd be able to resist her own desires.

Abby tried a playful giggle that sounded more like the desperate squeak of a field mouse fleeing from a hawk. When she tugged, trying to pull away from him, Mac held her.

"Tell me," he said. "Tell me what you're after."

Her training kicked in. She became one hundred percent Vanessa, tossing her platinum blond hair and fluttering her lashes. "I want a little excitement. I'm bored at this safe house."

"You want me to give you some excitement."

"Absolutely," she said. "Tomorrow, I want you to take me to Vail and buy me pretty things."

"Is that the whole truth?"

"Honey, you can't handle the truth."

"I remember that movie line," he said. "Things didn't turn out well for the liars."

"But this isn't a movie." Though she could have used a karate move to break his hold on her wrist, she was playing her part as Vanessa. She peeled his fingers open, one by one until she was free. "Until tomorrow, sleep well."

She darted into her own bedroom and closed the bathroom door. Sleep well? Hah! Abby fully expected to spend the whole night tossing and turning, trying to forget how great he looked in his towel. She was totally in lust over Mac Granger, the man she was supposed to be investigating.

Chapter Five

The next day, Mac was surprised to find himself on the way to Vail. He never thought Julia Last would agree to Vanessa's demand for a shopping excursion. He understood when Julia allowed the blonde sexbomb to visit the tavern in Redding; it wasn't likely a protected witness would run into someone who recognized her in a small, secluded Colorado town. But Vail was a different kind of community with visitors from all over the country, all over the world.

Though Julia appeared to be a by-the-book manager of the safe house, she'd given in to Vanessa's whining on the condition that they be accompanied by Roger Flannery, the young FBI agent who was driving the safe house SUV.

Vanessa sat beside Roger in the passenger seat. Mac was in the rear.

While Vanessa oohed and aahed over the mountain scenery and flirted with young Roger, Mac studied her. Under all that lipstick and eyeshadow, she had a glowing, natural beauty that came from good health and excellent physical conditioning. Neither of those traits were typical of a pampered Las Vegas showgirl who'd gotten involved with a notorious crime family. Nor did her intelligent vocabulary match his expectations for Vanessa Nye. Who was she?

She turned in her seat and tossed him a lively grin. "I want lobster for lunch."

"We're in the mountains," he pointed out. "Not the greatest place for seafood."

"But Roger says he knows a restaurant." She stroked the young man's arm. "I'm sure he knows his lobsters. Right?"

"It was just a suggestion," Roger said.

When Mac caught his gaze in the rearview mirror, the young agent quickly looked away. Was he embarrassed about being drawn into an unprofessional conversation with Vanessa? Or did he have something to hide?

Mac folded his arms across his chest and

slouched back in his seat. If he'd gotten to the point where he was suspecting babyfaced Roger Flannery, he must have turned into a paranoid nutcase who thought everybody was out to get him. *Crazy!* He should give it a rest. Just sit back and enjoy the rest of the damned day. A "gift" from the feds.

At Vail village, they parked underground and walked into town. A familiar route. When Mac was growing up, he'd spent a lot of time on Vail's winding, pedestrian-only streets. All through high school, he had worked here on weekends. Though the ski area had been built in the 1960s, the architecture resembled an old-time, quaint Alpine village.

"*Faux* Bavarian," Vanessa said. "It's cute, but why are all these people in lederhosen?"

"Oktoberfest," Mac said.

"But it's September."

"As good a time as any for drinking beer and eating bratwurst."

"Too many people," Roger muttered. He wore the wraparound dark glasses that seemed to be FBI issue for surveillance. No doubt this newbie agent was diligently scanning the crowds, looking for potential threats among the tourists, the accordion players and the German folk dancers who filled the town square.

Vanessa pointed up. "What's that?"

"The clock tower. It used to be the tallest structure in the village."

Beyond the clock tower and the covered bridge over Gore Creek was an unobstructed view of the ski slope. Over the years, the village itself had been surrounded by condos and towering hotel lodges, but it was still a pretty view.

Vanessa tugged at Mac's arm. "Polka?"

"I don't dance."

"Anybody can polka. Just follow the music. Oom-pah-pah. One-two-three. One big step, then two little ones."

He looked down at his feet. Inside his boots, his toes curled. "No way."

With a surprising show of strength, she dragged him into the dancing crowd. "One-two-three. One-two-three."

He had to move or be trampled. *Oom-pah-pah.* The easy rhythm bounced through his head. He was moving. *One-two-three.* Moving fast. Vanessa made it seem easy as she twirled lightly in his arms.

Round and round they went. The smiling faces in the crowd became a homogenized blur against the whitewashed buildings and peaked roofs and the towering slope. He concentrated on moving to the music. Dancing? He was dancing? And he was dangerously close to forgetting about his suspicions and having fun.

He hadn't felt so lighthearted in years. And it wasn't the music or the dancing or the spectacular setting. It was her. Vanessa was vivacious, funny and irresistibly adorable as she leaned back in his arms, laughing and encouraging him to go faster.

"You're smiling," she said.

"Am not." But he couldn't force a frown.

"There's nothing wrong with having a good time."

He knew that. More than once, the departmental shrink had advised him to lighten up. But the current of suppressed anger and sadness that flowed through Mac's veins was an occupational hazard for a homicide detective. He constantly saw humanity at its worst.

"You're a good dancer," Vanessa said.

Only with her in his arms. She was special. Beautiful. Mysterious. And more clever than was good for her. Or for him.

When they spun away from the other dancers, Roger appeared beside them. The young agent looked so tense that Mac almost felt sorry for him. "Take Vanessa for a whirl," Mac said. "Lighten up."

Roger stiffened. "I don't think—"

But Vanessa had already pulled him into the throng.

Mac stood back and watched with an unabashed grin on his face. There was no reason why they shouldn't take advantage of the celebration and have some fun like the rest of these weekday tourists. This was a festival, a time to guzzle dark beer and eat enough brats to clog every artery.

As Mac scanned the crowd, he saw someone familiar. That shouldn't be a big deal. Many of the people he grew up with, including his friend Jess, worked and lived in Vail. But this was a more recent acquaintance…someone he had never actually met.

Mac recognized Leo Fisher from the photograph Sheila had given him. The undercover FBI agent was hatless. His long brown hair was pulled back in a ponytail at his nape. He walked with a cane, recovering from the gunshot wound Mac had inflicted.

Before Mac could figure out how to reach Leo Fisher, Vanessa and Roger were back beside him. Leo had disappeared into the crowd.

Roger forced a scowl. "We can only stay here for one hour. Let's move along."

At the edge of the town square, Vanessa paused beside a posting of Oktoberfest events. "We can't leave before the bratwurst eating contest."

"You wanted lobster," Roger muttered. "And to shop."

"No need to remind me," she said. "I never forget shopping."

While Mac watched for another glimpse of Leo Fisher, Vanessa scanned the windows in the pricey boutiques. "Remember, Mac. You're buying."

"You should get decent boots," Mac suggested, glancing down at her ridiculously high-heeled shoes. "Boots that you can walk in."

"Lovely idea."

She linked her arm with his and dragged him into a shop. Roger followed and positioned himself so he could watch the front door.

While Vanessa tried on shoes, she snuggled

up to Mac. "Want to have an adventure?" she whispered.

"Define adventure," he said.

"Roger's driving me crazy with his body-guard routine. Let's ditch him."

"Why?"

"Come on." She nudged his arm. "Don't you ever get the urge to misbehave? Besides, it'll be good experience for Special Agent Flannery to try and find us."

For a moment, Mac considered. This whole trip to Vail smacked of a setup. It was entirely possible that she had a meet scheduled with Leo Fisher.

However, if he wanted to uncover her motives, he ought to agree with her scheme. "Sure. Let's do it."

Vanessa laid out the plan. She'd go into the back room to try on an outfit, then slip out the back door. Mac would make up an excuse to go out the front door. They'd meet on the corner.

Mac followed her plan, giving Roger a quick nod. "I'm going to step outside for a breath of air."

"She's really some kind of woman," Roger said.

"Oh, yeah." *Some kind of trouble.*

"I mean, when she first showed up at the safe house, she was all slutty. But she's really smart."

Too smart for her own good? Mac stepped outside. "I'll be back in a minute."

When he saw Vanessa on the corner, Mac was relieved. It had crossed his mind that she might take this opportunity to escape from custody as a protected witness. But why? What would that prove? The feds were there to protect her.

Her eyes shone with a mischievous spark. "Let's go this way."

The village was small, but the winding streets and the Oktoberfest crowd created a lot of hiding places. They neared the chair-lift where tourists took round-trip rides up the snowless mountain. "I used to work here," Mac said.

"Running the lift?"

"A great job for the summer," he said. "And better in the winter, when I could ski for free."

She cocked her head to one side. "Under that jaded facade, you really are a mountain man, aren't you?"

"Used to be."

She glanced over her shoulder. "There's Roger behind us. We should go the other way."

Even in her high heels, her movements were quick yet subtle enough not to attract attention. Mac had the sense that she knew a thing or two about surveillance. "This isn't the first time you've done this."

"You're right." She grinned like a teenager. "I don't like having a keeper. I know the agents are watching me for my own good, but... ugh!"

"Being a protected witness isn't a game."

"It's boring," she said. "And if we're going to keep hiding from Roger, I need a hat to cover this hair. It makes me stand out in a crowd."

"It's more than the hair."

"Ooh, Mac. Was that a compliment? How sweet."

They ducked into a shop where Mac paid way too much for a simple knitted hat. Then they were back on the streets.

If Mac hadn't spotted Leo before, he might have enjoyed this little game. They were playing hide-and-seek like a couple of kids.

Vanessa leaned close to him. "You don't usually break the rules, do you?"

"Never."

She pulled him into a doorway. "Having fun?"

He wanted to say yes and give her what she wanted, everything she wanted. Her glowing enthusiasm was far more seductive than when she was being outrageously sexy. "Are you trying to lead me astray?"

"That's the idea," she said. "We're partners in crime. Or spies. Like James Bond."

When he looked away from her, he saw the real thing—an FBI undercover agent, Leo Fisher. He was less than ten yards away. Standing near the clock tower, he appeared to be waiting for someone. Vanessa? Was he waiting for her?

Mac hated the idea that she might have a hidden agenda, but he had to test this theory. "See that guy over there? The one with the cane and the ponytail?"

She bobbed her head. "I see him."

"As long as we're pretending to be spies, let's follow him."

"You mean like surveillance?"

"Right."

"Why him?"

Mac shrugged, worried that his expression would give away his real motivation. "Why not?"

"Okay." She ducked her head. "We'll sneak up really close to him."

As they mingled with the crowd, edging closer to Leo Fisher, Mac watched Vanessa for any sign of recognition. In a moment, they were standing directly behind Leo's back. Mac felt a bit foolish, sneaking up on the man he'd accidentally shot. He and Leo were both in law enforcement, both on the same side. Or were they?

Leo met the person he was waiting for. They exchanged a few words and walked away. Mac distinctly heard him speak a name: Nicholas Dirk. "Did you hear that?" he asked Vanessa.

"Dirk?"

"Nicholas Dirk."

As Leo and his companion moved away, Roger appeared beside them. Behind his dark glasses, his face flushed beet-red. "What the hell are you doing?"

"There you are," Vanessa said. "Really, Roger. You shouldn't wander off like that."

"But you're the one who…" He threw up his hands. "Forget it! We're leaving."

"Please, Roger. Just another couple of minutes."

Another person detached from the crowd and came toward them. "Hey, Mac."

It was Jess. After a quick hug, Mac introduced him to Roger.

"And I remember Vanessa," Jess said with the smooth charm that came second nature to him. "I thought I saw you in the square. Dancing."

"I got Mac to dance," she said. "He's a natural."

Jess cocked a skeptical eyebrow. "Mac? He didn't even dance at his own wedding."

"You were married?" Vanessa asked.

"A long time ago." Mac glanced toward Roger, who was obviously aggravated. He looked like a cartoon character with steam shooting out of his ears. "We probably should get going."

"I'll walk you to your car," Jess said.

While Vanessa chatted with Roger, Mac fell into step beside Jess. He purposely hung back a few paces so Roger and Vanessa couldn't overhear their conversation.

"Jess, do you know anybody named Nicholas Dirk?"

"Yeah." Jess frowned. "I know Dirk."

"You don't like him."

"A gut feeling," Jess said. "I've got no real reason to dislike the man. He's really rich."

"What's his field?"

"Land development, something like that. Every year he donates a ton of money to the ski patrol, which is why I know him. Dirk has this huge chalet, and he throws big parties every weekend."

"Do you go to these parties?"

"As a member of the ski patrol, I've got a standing invite." His frown deepened. "Why the questions?"

"I'm not sure," Mac said honestly. "It's probably nothing. What if I wanted to go to one of these parties?"

"No problem. I could arrange it." He shot Mac a sidelong glance. "There's something else you should know about Dirk. He used to date Lisa Hammond."

She'd been Mac's high school sweetheart—a pretty blonde who taught skiing and snowboarding. Tall and slim with legs that went on forever. A goddess in blue jeans. Lisa was the first girl he'd made love to, but he definitely wasn't her first man. Lisa was a little too wild for Mac's taste. "There's a name I haven't heard in years. Does Lisa still live up here?"

Jess nodded. "With her daughter. Nicholas Dirk is the father."

A sharp pain snapped inside Mac's head. If Dirk turned out to be a bad guy, he didn't want to think of Lisa being held in his clutches. "Does she live with him?"

"They never married," Jess said, "but Dirk gave her a condo and pays child support."

That was the decent thing to do. Apparently, Dirk wasn't a total scumbag. Why was Leo Fisher interested in him?

LATER THAT AFTERNOON, Sheila picked up the precinct phone at her desk. It was Mac, calling on his cell phone.

"Busy?" he asked.

"I'm at my desk, shuffling papers," she grumbled. "How come you get a vacation in the mountains, and I'm stuck here?"

"I got shot," he said.

"Next time, I want to be the one with an injury."

"That could be arranged," he said coolly. "I have a little project for you."

"Wait a minute. I thought you agreed that you wouldn't investigate."

"It's just a question."

She exhaled an impatient sigh as she pushed a stack of file folders across her cluttered desktop. "What is it?"

"I want you to talk to Vince Elliot."

"Fine," she snapped. Actually, this request wouldn't be a problem for Sheila. She liked Vince. He was kind of scruffy but had a very cute butt.

"Ask him if he knows a guy in Vail named Nicholas Dirk. Then give me a call back on my cell."

"Whatever."

Sheila disconnected the call and glared at the phone. The way Mac treated her—like she was some kind of moron—really grated on her nerves. Hadn't she warned him to back off on investigating?

She reached for her latte and took a sip, wishing it was whiskey. Where did Mac get the right to give her assignments? She was under no obligation to do his dirty work. On the other hand, a little chat with Vince Elliot might work to her advantage.

She tracked down the vice cop at his desk

and perched on the edge, giving him an outstanding view of her long legs. "Mac called."

Vince allowed his gaze to linger on her thighs before he looked up at her face. "And?"

"He asked me to ask you about a guy. Nicholas Dirk."

"Damn it." Abruptly, Vince pushed his chair away from his desk. "Don't get me wrong, Sheila. I know Mac saved my butt at that warehouse shoot-out, and I'm grateful. But what the hell is he doing?"

"Beats me." This was her opportunity to make Mac look bad, and she grabbed it. "He's been acting weird, you know. Like he's got some big secret or something."

"What kind of secret?"

She shrugged. "Maybe you and I should get together after work, maybe have a drink and talk about Mac."

"No, thanks." He stood. "You tell Mac that he's messing around with things that are none of his business."

"Sure, Vince. I'll tell him."

"He needs to get out of the way." His voice lowered. "Before somebody decides to take him out."

As Vince walked away, she admired his

broad shoulders and that totally adorable ass. When this was all over, Sheila thought that she maybe ought to transfer to vice.

Chapter Six

After dinner at the safe house, Abby watched television in the great room with the other residents and agents. Roger was still angry with her, and she couldn't blame him. Sneaking away at Oktoberfest had been a mean trick, but she'd wanted to get Mac on her side. How had he put it? *To lead him astray.*

During their romp in Vail, they had bonded. Mac saw her as a buddy. While they were dodging into the boutiques and hiding in doorways, she had felt the companionship building between them.

And then, out of the blue, there was Leo. Abby shuddered at the memory. It had taken all her undercover training to keep from showing any sign of recognition when Mac picked Leo Fisher, her former fiancé, out of the crowd. When she and Mac had sidled up close, she'd been scared to death that Leo would turn around and identify her.

But all that had emerged was a name. Nicholas Dirk. The drug lord that Leo was determined to nab? *Not my problem.* Mac was her focus. And he seemed to be hiding out in his room.

Saying her good-nights to the others, she went upstairs to her bedroom. Was Mac purposely avoiding her? She listened at the bathroom door and heard nothing. Was he sleeping?

When she washed her face and brushed her teeth, she made a lot of noise in the hope that he'd appear from his side of the bathroom. Her instincts told her the time was ripe to offer Mac a bribe.

But she didn't want to. On some level, she didn't want this assignment to be over.

That didn't make any sense at all. Why on earth would she want to keep up this pretense? In her bedroom, Abby wriggled out of her skintight clothing, and exhaled a heartfelt sigh of relief. She was tired; flouncing around like a former showgirl was hard work. Even her breasts were exhausted after spending all day in a push-up bra. The sooner this assignment was over, the better.

Discarding her leather slacks and leopard-patterned top, she pulled on a comfy, warm pair of red thermal underwear. Her gaze wandered toward the bathroom door. Too easily, she imagined Mac standing at the sink, wearing only a towel. A lovely warmth coiled through her. She didn't want the assignment to end because she was enjoying, really enjoying, her time with Mac. Teasing him was fun. Matching wits was a challenge.

She flung herself down on top of the down comforter. With her arms stretched out, she could span the bed but there was plenty of room left over for a Denver homicide cop who was born and raised in the mountains. Why had he left this idyllic place? What had drawn him to the city?

She wished they could erase their suspicions and talk to each other honestly, to reveal their deepest secrets. The constant deception of her work left her yearning for the truth. She wanted to hear Mac speak her real name, wanted to see his eyes not veiled by doubt.

There was a tap on the bathroom door. "Vanessa?"

I'm Abby. My name is Abby Nelson. "Come in, Mac."

The door handle rattled. "It's locked."

She leaped from the bed, twisted the latch and opened the door wide. "Welcome."

His gaze swept over her, and he grinned.

"What's so funny?" she asked.

"You don't strike me as the type of woman who wears thermal underwear to bed."

"Sometimes, it's better to be warm than sexy."

He stared at her face with such intensity that she had to glance away for fear that he would see right through her.

"You look different," he said. "Younger. I even see a couple of freckles."

This was her real face, unguarded. Quickly, she remembered that she was a professional undercover agent, highly trained. Her job was to find out if Mac was open to a bribe. "I know why you're here, Mac."

"Yeah?"

"You're suspicious of me," she said. "You have been from the first time we met. And, I'm ready to tell you that you're right. I'm not what I appear to be."

"Who are you?"

So many times before, he'd asked that question. And she'd answered with one lie after another. "I'm not a mindless bimbo, Mac. Not just a trophy."

"Go on," he encouraged.

Looking him straight in the face, she lied, "I'm much higher up in the Santoro family than anyone knows. After I testify, I fully intend to take over the business."

"The Santoro business?" His eyebrows lifted. She could tell that he hadn't expected this twist. "Let me get this straight. You intend to take over an international crime family."

"Are you surprised?"

Though he tried to maintain a poker face, she could see his confusion. And his disappointment. "I know you're a smart woman, Vanessa. But you're talking about a major operation. A business."

"There might be a place in my organization for a man like you." Praying that he'd turn her down, she continued, "If you play your cards right, I'd consider you as someone who might run my Denver operations. You could make a lot of money. More importantly, you would become a very powerful man."

"You're offering me a job."

An array of unspoken signals flashed across his face. A downward turn to his mouth. A tension at the edge of his eyes. He was angry...and still suspicious of her.

"Trust me," she said. "You won't be sorry."

"I'm a cop," he reminded her.

"Exactly. When I set up shop in Denver, I'll need an inside edge. I want to know who runs the drug trade."

"I'm homicide. Not vice."

"But you know people." She braced her fists on her hips, throwing down the challenge. "A guy like you must have connections."

"You think I'm already on the take."

"Whatever they're paying you, I'll double it."

"That's a hell of an offer."

Mac turned away from her. He recognized the game she was playing. She had blatantly offered him a bribe and accused him of having criminal contacts. Her act was too pat, and he wasn't buying it. The future head of the Santoro crime family? No way! Though he didn't know who she was working for, he was certain that Vanessa had been sent here to test him. She was undercover.

And every word she spoke was a lie. Of all the women who had betrayed him, she was the worst. And she would pay for her deception.

Turning to face her, he made a challenge of his own. "If I accept this offer, would I also have you?"

"What do you mean?"

"I want you to be my lover, Vanessa."

Though her expression remained unchanged, her body flinched. Her muscles tensed. How far would she go in this charade?

He added more pressure. "If we're working together, we should be close."

"I really don't think—"

"Don't think."

He pulled her into his arms. Before she could object, his lips claimed hers. He meant to test her, to force her out of her lies. But the effect of her body pressed against his evoked a whole different response. She excited him. Her breasts rubbed against his chest. Her legs twined with his. Damn it! He didn't want to be aroused.

Fortunately, she ended their kiss quickly, pushing against his chest. "Back off."

"Playing hard to get," he said through clenched teeth. "Is that the way Santoro liked it?"

"Give me an answer, Mac. Will you work with me? Be my man in Denver. Give me all your contacts."

More lies. So many lies that he couldn't fathom the depth of her dishonesty. His arms fell away from her. In disgust, he turned away and left the room.

THE NEXT DAY, Mac still couldn't figure her out. "Everything she told me," he said, "every word was a lie."

"Are you sure?" Jess exited from the highway near Vail. They were on their way to take a look at the mountain chalet owned by Nicholas Dirk. "Vanessa doesn't seem like a liar to me."

"Because she's really good at it."

Barely able to contain his frustration and rage, Mac glared through the passenger side window of Jess's Jeep as they drove past rows of high-priced, luxury condominiums. It was a warm, sunny day, but he saw only gloom. He hated liars, especially a lying, manipulative woman like Vanessa…or whatever her real name was.

Her phony bribe put her at the head of the posse of those who suspected him. He couldn't believe this was happening. Not to him, damn it. He was a good cop. Before the shooting at the warehouse, he hadn't been aware of having so many enemies. Sure, there were a couple of grudges among co-workers and misdirected hatred from suspects in homicide investigations. But he'd never before had this feeling that everybody was out to get him.

Jess shook his head. "I can't believe your lousy track record with women."

"All men aren't like you," Mac grumbled. "Most of us don't date movie stars."

"Tell me why you think Vanessa is lying."

"Number one, she arranged to be at the place where I'm staying." Mac ticked off the reasons on his fingers. "Number two, as soon as I met her, she started coming on to me. Shoving her cleavage in my face and shaking her tail."

"Maybe because she liked you," Jess suggested.

"Number three, she offered me a bribe." He held up his fourth finger. "Last but not least, she made reference to my supposed criminal connections in Denver. If I'd accepted her offer, it would prove that I'm a dirty cop."

"Why would anybody think that?"

"Because I shot and killed a drug dealer who was about to turn snitch."

"You were framed?"

"Must be, but I'll be damned if I can figure out how or why. I thought I was just in the wrong place at the wrong time."

Mac was determined to prove that the suspicions of him were unfounded. From what Sheila had told him on the phone, Vince Elliot had reacted to Nicholas Dirk's name. Dirk had to be one of the bad guys. "Did you get me invited to Dirk's weekend party?"

"No problem. I talked to one of his guys yesterday. They said any friend of mine was a friend of theirs. What do you think Dirk has to do with this?"

"Drugs."

Jess shook his head in disbelief. "I've never caught a whiff of illegal substances around him."

"Because you're not a narc."

Frankly, neither was Mac. When it came to homicide investigations, his work ranked among the best. But those cases were a matter of piecing together evidence and following a trail. The work of a narcotics investigation required a whole different set of skills, most especially an ability to conceal, cajole and deceive—talents that made him think of Vanessa. Without hesitation, she had looked him in the eye and lied. How far would she have gone? Would she have made love with him to prove her case? He hated to think that the sexual heat generated between them was faked.

"Here's the place," Jess said as he pulled over and parked on the shoulder of the road. He pointed through a stone archway toward a massive Bavarian chalet-style facade. "Nicholas Dirk's humble abode."

In addition to peaked eaves and half a dozen chimneys, the house seemed to climb up the hillside where it was nestled amid thick forest. "Is that all one house?"

"It's huge," Jess said. "Home theater, bowling lane, exercise room and indoor basketball court. You name it, Dirk's got it."

"What about security?"

"Oh, yeah. In fact, you could lean out the window right now and wave to the camera."

"Wow."

"No kidding," Jess said. "Dirk has maids, a chauffeur, a secretary and a full-time staff of five or six guys."

Overwhelmed, Mac sank back in the passenger seat. How the hell could he penetrate those defenses? He didn't have a plan, didn't have backup. His only resource came from a deep motivation to prove himself innocent. Somehow, that would have to be enough.

"What comes next?" Jess asked. "Do we storm the castle?"

"I don't know where to start," Mac admitted. "When I'm working homicide, I flash my badge and demand the truth. But this?"

"What are you looking for?"

"A dirty cop," Mac said. "Everybody seems sure that there's a cop on the take. I need to prove it's not me."

Jess slipped his Jeep into gear and eased onto the two-lane road. "Maybe you should talk to Paul about this."

"No way. Paul's like me—a straightforward cop. This investigation is going to be complicated. There's an FBI undercover agent involved. And Denver vice."

"Ow," Jess said. "What makes you think you can figure this out when they can't?"

"I don't know." But he couldn't just sit back and watch while his whole life, everything he'd worked for, went up in flames. "You're right about one thing. I need to think. Let's go to the rapids."

"You're on." Jess grinned. "I haven't been there in years."

When they were in high school, the rapids had been a favorite hideout. In a secluded canyon off the main road, it was a beautiful spot with huge boulders overlooking the narrows of Gore Creek. A great place to take a girlfriend. And an even better place to hang out with the guys. Mac, Jess and Paul had spent many a summer day sprawled on the rocks like lizards in the sun, then diving into the cool, churning waters.

Following back roads, they drove deep into the forested hillsides. The ride should have been relaxing, but Mac's gut twisted in a tight knot. "I've got to investigate. To prove that I haven't done anything wrong."

"I believe you," Jess said.

Mac glanced toward his handsome friend. "You don't have a choice. You have to say you believe me, pal."

"Or else what?"

"I'll kick your sorry ass."

"Not a chance," Jess said. "I'm in way better shape than you are."

"But I'm tougher."

"But not always smarter." Jess's voice turned serious. "Do you mind if I give you some solid advice?"

"Is there anything I can say to stop you?"

"Not really."

Mac sighed. "What is it?"

"If Nicholas Dirk is really some kind of drug kingpin who has outsmarted the feds and Denver vice, don't go after him by yourself. Let somebody else sort it out."

"What if they don't?"

That was Mac's fear. The suspicions directed toward him seemed impossible. Yet, he was a suspect. What if the truth was never known?

Jess parked at a wide spot along a dirt road, and they climbed out of the Jeep. When they were younger, they'd raced along the narrow path through tall pines and giant boulders. Now, they walked quietly, thinking and listening to the rush of water in the creek. The path separated from the creek and ascended to a ridge along arid hillside.

"We should be careful," Jess said. "It's open season on small game. There might be hunters in the area."

"Do we look like rabbits?"

"To a guy with a six-pack and a rifle? Yeah."

Hunting accidents occurred with regularity in the mountains, and Mac reminded himself that the beauty of the mountains hid a thousand hazards.

After about a hundred yards, they emerged from the pine forest and stepped onto a massive, flat-topped boulder. Below them, the creek narrowed into churning white-water rapids.

"I can't believe we used to dive off here," Jess said. "That's got to be at least fifteen feet."

"That was a hell of a long time ago."

Mac rubbed his shoulder. Though the wound was healing, he still felt an ache. His body had aged. He carried the scars of many accidents and mistaken judgments. He was older. But wiser?

Maybe Jess had the right idea. Mac should leave the investigating to somebody else. A wise man wouldn't strike out on his own. A wise man would trust that the false accusations would be discredited. For sure, a wise man wouldn't be distracted by the likes of Vanessa Nye.

Mac heard a mechanical click—the unmistakable sound of a gun being cocked. He turned and stared. Among the lodgepole pines at the edge of the forest, a lone gunman in hunting gear leveled a rifle. He wasn't aiming at game. The bore of his weapon pointed directly at them.

Chapter Seven

Acting on instinct, Mac dodged toward Jess and grabbed his arm, trying to pull him out of the way to protect him.

Jess shrugged off his grasp. "What the hell are you doing?"

"Get down," Mac ordered.

Jess spotted the threat. Instead of ducking, he waved his arms at the hunter. "Hey, you. Don't shoot. We're not rabbits."

The blast from the rifle echoed in the rocky canyon. Jess was hit. He staggered back a pace. His knees buckled.

Before Mac could reach him, Jess toppled from the edge of their rocky perch and fell into the churning water below. Mac had no choice but to dive in after him. As he leaped, he heard another rifle shot.

His plummet into the ice-cold water of

Gore Creek stunned his senses. He couldn't tell if he'd broken his legs in the fall because his entire body was immediately numb. Frantically, he paddled, struggling to stay in one place. "Jess! Where are you?"

He'd lost Jess, couldn't see him anywhere. This water was deep and fast. Jess could be at the bottom, held down by the current.

Mac dove. He tried to keep his eyes open, but it was no use. He couldn't see. The rapids dragged him downstream. He fought his way to the surface and came up gasping.

There was Jess. Clinging to a rock. The front of his white shirt was pink with diluted blood. He'd been shot in the chest.

Fighting the currents, Mac reached Jess and held him, keeping his head up. The water swept Mac's feet out from under him. Together, he and Jess were tossed like driftwood on the surging white waves.

Mac saw the boulder before they hit. He felt the impact in his injured shoulder. And his head. He'd taken a hard whack to the skull. There was a flash of pitch-dark behind his eyelids. No! He couldn't pass out. He had to get Jess out of this water.

Using all his strength, he dragged Jess to

the water's edge. The current whirled and eddied around them, but they made it, slogging into the thick underbrush.

He looked up, expecting to see the hunter. If the gunman stood on their perch, he'd be able pick them off. They were easy targets. Helpless.

But the hunter didn't appear.

Instead, he heard an exchange of gunfire. What the hell was going on? There was the shout of a woman's voice. Vanessa?

Mac saw her running through the trees. She wore the knit cap he'd bought for her yesterday. It was pulled down low on her forehead like a helmet. A warrior's helmet. She stopped, braced herself and expertly aimed her handgun to fire.

"Mac, what happened?" Jess spoke slowly. His eyes were dazed. "How did we get wet?"

"Hunters," Mac said.

"I told you so."

His eyelids closed. Blood seeped from his chest wound, staining his white shirt.

From years in homicide, Mac had seen death a hundred times. But not Jess. Not his old friend. The pain Mac felt had nothing to do with his injuries from being buffeted in the rapids. His soul ached.

Vanessa charged down the hillside toward them. Without a word, she helped Mac pull Jess all the way out of the water.

"Did you get him?" Mac asked. "The guy who shot at us?"

"I might have winged him. He's retreating."

Mac looked helplessly at Jess. "He's still breathing."

"Neither one of you look good," she said. "We need to get you both to a hospital."

Supporting Jess between them, they climbed a path up the hillside and through the forest. There was a road back here he'd never seen before. Parked on the shoulder was the SUV from the safe house.

With Vanessa's help, he loaded Jess into the back seat and sat beside him, cradling his unconscious body, willing his heart to keep pumping. *Don't die. Please, Jess. Please, don't die.*

Behind the wheel, Vanessa drove with speed and determination. They jostled over the rough back roads. Over her shoulder, she said, "Try to find a blanket back there. You're probably both in shock."

Mac groped behind the seats but found nothing. The cold from the icy water had seeped into his bones. His hands were tingling and clumsy. He wasn't thinking right.

"Can't find anything." He focused on Jess and the spreading flow of blood. The wound was high and on the left side, away from Jess's heart. "I've got to stop the bleeding."

"Apply pressure to the wound." Without slowing the vehicle, she tore off her leopard-patterned jacket. "Use this. Put it over the wound, press down and try to staunch the flow."

Mac did as she said. Carefully he pressed down. Below the skin and muscle, he felt the bones give. "His ribs."

"Don't press hard," she cautioned. "If his ribs are broken, you'll do more damage. We shouldn't have moved him."

"There was no choice."

If they had waited for a rescue unit, Jess would have bled to death. It was ironic that the one person in the car who would have known the correct first aid procedures was Jess—a well-trained member of the ski patrol who knew how to rescue and stabilize injured skiers.

"I should have spotted the shooter," Vanessa said as she swung a hard left. The tires of the SUV hit paved road. "He came out of nowhere."

"Not a hunter," Mac replied. "He was dressed like one, but he was aiming at us."

"Did you recognize him?"

"No." All Mac saw was the rifle.

"I'm sorry, Mac. I'm sorry for everything."

"Tell me one thing. Who the hell are you?"

"My name is Abby," she said. "FBI Special Agent Abigail Nelson. I'm working undercover."

He was right about her, but that wasn't important. Not anymore. The only thing that counted was getting Jess to the hospital in time to save his life.

Though he was dazed, Mac knew they were flying as she made a high-speed merge onto the highway. She drove better and faster than an ambulance. At the same time, she juggled her cell phone.

Her voice seemed far away as she called in the emergency. He heard her mention Jess's name. She snapped the cell phone closed. "They're waiting for us at the E.R."

He leaned close to his old friend's pallid

face. The blood had drained from his complexion. His cheeks were slack. "Hang on, buddy. You'll make it. You've got to make it."

Jess's eyelids fluttered open. "Who shot me?"

"I don't know."

"Had to happen." He exhaled in a soft wheeze. "Sooner or later."

"Why? Is somebody after you?"

"Lots of angry ex-boyfriends."

His bloodless lips parted in a weak smile.

Mac doubted the attack had anything to do with his friend's glamorous love life. That hunter had been after him. Jess had just gotten in the way.

FOLLOWING DIRECTIONS from her indispensible GPS locator, Abby reached the hospital in record time. Every second was important; Jess had lost a lot of blood.

At the emergency entrance, the E.R. staff charged out the door to meet her, and she was glad that she'd called ahead. Jess Isler was a popular guy in Vail, especially here at the hospital where his work put him in contact with these people. With incredible speed, he was lifted onto a gurney and whisked inside.

Her prayers went with him. It was so wrong that he'd been shot, that he might be near death.

She turned her attention to Mac. He nearly fell getting out of the car, but he staggered forward, waving away the offers of assistance.

Abby could see his determination to stay with his friend no matter what. She edged up beside him. "Let's have somebody look at your injuries."

"I'm fine," he growled.

His clothes were wet and stained with Jess's blood. Shivers wracked his body, and the hair on the back of his head was matted with blood. Likely, he had a concussion or was on the verge of shock. "You look like hell, Mac."

"Been a rough day." He lurched toward the counter in the emergency room and leaned heavily against it. "I'm Jess Isler's friend. Where did you take him?"

A gray-haired nurse with the leathery tan of an avid outdoorswoman glared at Mac. "He's in the operating room."

"Where's that?"

"You're not allowed in that area." She

came around the counter and firmly gripped his upper arm. "Come with me, young man."

He yanked away from her. "Don't worry about me. I'm fine. It's Jess. He's—"

"Being taken care of," the nurse said. "You're a bit unsteady on your feet. Have you been drinking?"

"Hell, no."

Abby spoke to the nurse. "He took a fall into Gore Creek. He's probably in shock."

"That could explain the hostile attitude," the nurse said. "Oxygen deprivation to the brain."

Abby added, "He might also have a concussion."

"Don't listen to her," Mac roared. Any semblance of his self-control vanished. He was over the top—way over the top. His arms flailed, pushing away imaginary enemies. He glared at Abby. "You're a liar."

If the situation with Jess hadn't been so potentially tragic, she might have snapped back at him. But now? He wasn't himself. She tried to get closer to him. "I'm on your side, Mac."

He squinted at her. Too loudly, he accused, "You're out to get me. Everybody's out to get me."

"Paranoia," the nurse said. "Another symptom of shock."

But Mac wasn't making up these threats. Abby reached out and touched his arm. "I'd never hurt you. Or Jess."

As he gazed down at her, his features softened. His lower lip trembled. Raw vulnerability shone through his eyes, and she longed to reassure him with a promise that everything would be all right. But she couldn't. Not even Abby—trained in deception—could tell such an impossibly huge lie. Jess might die. Mac was in deep trouble; someone had tried to kill him.

"Let's go, Mac. You need to see a doctor."

"I'm fine. Great!" He stumbled away from her, weaving as if he were walking a tightrope. His arms waved as he tried to gain his balance. "Where's Jess?"

Three more hospital personnel in scrubs appeared near the counter. They spread out and circled Mac.

Like a wounded mountain lion, he snarled at them. "Back off! I want to know what you're doing to my friend."

"The doctors are working on Jess," Abby said. "There's nothing you can do."

"Blood," Mac said. He tried to roll up his sleeve. "I can give blood. Or a kidney. I'd give Jess a kidney, damn it."

When Abby reached out again to touch his arm and calm him down, he dodged. His back was against the wall.

"Listen up." She spoke sharply, hoping her words would penetrate his confusion. "You need to cooperate with these people. They're here to help you."

"Is that another one of your lies?" Mac glanced toward a man in navy-blue scrubs. "She's a conman."

He grinned at Abby's cleavage. "She doesn't look like any man I've ever seen."

"It's all a front." Mac's bravado was fading fast. He tried to glare at her, but his eyes wavered. He lifted a finger to point at her. "She's pretty, though. Real pretty."

His knees bent. In slow motion, he slid down the wall.

AN HOUR and a half later, Mac was tucked into a bed in the intensive care unit. He'd been scanned and X-rayed and hooked up to IVs and a monitor that showed a reassuringly normal heartbeat.

Throughout these processes, Abby had stayed close to him. Not only was she concerned about his minor concussion and bruises, but she worried about his physical safety. She couldn't leave him unprotected. Not while somebody wanted him dead.

Standing at his bedside, she stared down at the rugged planes of his face. His dark blond hair, which was usually neatly combed, sprouted in all directions. Though the color in his face was much better, he seemed uncomfortable. His eyelids twitched, struggling to open. More than once, he'd pulled off the oxygen cannula. Obviously, he wanted to be up and active.

She stroked his warm forehead. "Hush, Mac."

It was far better for him to stay asleep until he was strong enough to handle this dire situation. Jess was still in surgery, and she'd heard no details about his condition.

Thus far, she had avoided talking to the sheriff, saying that this was probably a hunting accident. Of course, that was a lie. But what else could she do? An explanation of her undercover identity would surely compromise the FBI safe house. And she didn't have other information. She didn't know why Mac was on that road, didn't know who wanted to kill him.

Only one conclusion was clear to Abby. She had blown this assignment. Her shining record as an undercover agent was about to be dragged through the muck and mire. She'd made the most common rooky mistake—getting too involved with the subject of her inquiry. Her empathy for Mac showed a complete lack of professional detachment.

She looked up to see Paul Hemmings, clad in his brown deputy uniform, coming through the door into the ICU. His huge presence expanded and filled the entire unit. His thick eyebrows pulled down in a ferocious scowl. He was angry. Great! Just what she needed was another confrontation with a crazed mountain man.

Paul came directly to Mac's bedside. He took his friend's limp hand and squeezed. "Is he going to be all right?"

"The doctors seem to think so." She recited the list of injuries. "They gave him some kind of sedative, but he's fighting it off, trying to wake up. Have you heard anything about Jess?"

"He's busted up pretty bad, but the doc says he's strong. He'll make it. He's got to make it." Paul wheeled around to face her. "Did you tell the nurse that you were Mac's long-lost sister?"

She wouldn't have been allowed in ICU if she hadn't been a family member. "I might have said that."

"And your name is Abigail Nelson?"

"It is."

"Not Vanessa?"

"Not today."

"Mac said you were a liar." His voice rumbled inside his barrel chest. "We don't need you here. Get out."

She'd had enough of being pushed around by these macho guys. Yes, she'd lied to Mac. But she was only doing her job, and she didn't owe anybody an apology.

Instead of tucking her tail between her legs and slinking out the door, she took a step closer to Paul. Her head tilted back as she looked up at the big man. "I'm staying."

"Mac won't want to see you. I'm damn sure of that."

"Then let him tell me."

"Don't make me throw you out."

She squared her shoulders, her fingers drew into fists and her muscles tensed. She had no intention of getting into a physical showdown in ICU. But if push came to shove, Abby knew she could take this big man down. Her body language communicated that confidence. "I'm not leaving."

"Let her stay."

The sound of Mac's voice surprised them both. Paul leaned over the bed on one side. Abby dashed around the foot of the bed and stood on the opposite side beside the heart monitor, which had begun to beep faster.

Mac glanced up at her, then turned his head toward Paul. "No use in fighting her. She'll only be more stubborn."

Paul gripped Mac's hand. "How are you doing?"

"I'm okay. Jess?"

"Touch and go." Concern was written on the big man's face. "One thing is for damn sure…he's going to miss the first day of skiing this year."

With a groan, Mac pulled himself up to a sitting position, dislodging a sensor. On the monitor, his heartbeat went flat and made a shrill noise. "I want out of here."

"Forget it," Paul said. "You need—"

"Don't tell me what I need."

Abby stepped back to watch. Mac's previous aggressive behavior had been symptomatic of shock. This time, it was his own cranky, cynical personality shining through. He wasn't the type of man who could sit back and allow someone else to take care of him. Not when there was a battle to be fought.

Paul rumbled, "Lie down."

"I'm fine." Mac already had one leg out of the bed. "Where are my clothes?"

A nurse bustled into the room. She pushed Paul aside and jabbed a finger against Mac's chest. "Get back in that bed, Mister. And I mean now."

Mac held up his hands, warding her off. "Everything is okay. I'm ready to be released."

"If you don't lie down, I will have you restrained."

"Did you hear that?" Paul asked. "Mac, you'd better do what the nurse says. We've got enough to worry about without you acting like a jerk."

"But I'm fine."

"You'll still be fine tomorrow," Paul said

reasonably as he pushed Mac back into the bed. As soon as his head hit the pillow, he sighed. His eyelids slammed shut.

Paul turned toward Abby. "You stay with him. I'm going to see if there's any word on Jess."

As Paul lumbered out the door, the nurse repositioned the sensor for the heart monitor. Once again, there was a steady beep. To Abby, she said, "We'll be moving him up to a room very soon. After a good night's sleep, he ought to be fine."

With everyone else gone, Abby settled herself at Mac's bedside. There had already been one attempt on his life. She'd make certain there wasn't another.

"Abby," he said. "That's right, isn't it? Abby Nelson."

She felt a little glow of pleasure. It was nice to hear him call her by her real name. "That's right."

"And you're a fed."

"Right again."

"I want to get the guy who shot Jess." His eyes opened a slit. "And you're going to help me."

"Whatever you need."

This might be the most foolish decision she'd ever made, but she couldn't say no. She'd be there for him. No matter what.

Chapter Eight

The next morning, Abby sat beside Mac's bed in a private hospital room. On her lap, she held a paperback romance novel that she was unable to read. The words blurred together on the page. Her mind couldn't comprehend more than a phrase before skipping off the track.

Last night, she'd stood beside Mac while he gave a statement to the sheriff. Mac had said this was a hunting accident, and he didn't recognize the shooter. Clearly, he'd been lying. But the sheriff accepted Mac at his word and didn't push.

She knew why Mac hadn't told the truth. He wanted to pursue this investigation on his own. And he wanted her to help him. She'd do it. Even though she might be committing professional suicide.

When she'd offered Mac a bribe, her assignment was over, and she wasn't authorized to do more. Her boundaries were clear. To step outside those parameters meant disobeying her orders.

"Good morning, Abby."

This morning, he didn't look like a man who had been in medical crisis. His blue eyes were clear and alert as he pushed the button to make his bed rise to a sitting position.

"All things considered," she said, "you look good."

"It's the outfit," he said, rubbing at the cotton gown that covered his broad chest. "Close the door. We need to talk."

She did as he said and returned to sit on the bed beside his outstretched legs. "I suppose you want to know why I was posing as Vanessa Nye."

"First, tell me about Jess."

"The bullet punctured his lung and nicked a couple of organs. There was internal bleeding. He also has broken ribs. He's going to be off his feet for a while, but the good news is that he'll recover."

Mac leaned back against his pillows. His blue eyes darkened. "It was my fault."

"You didn't pull the trigger, Mac."

"I might as well have."

"Don't even start with the blame game," she said. "You're a cop. A professional. You know better."

If every incident in law enforcement was reduced to blame, the guilt would be over-whelming. Though Abby had never actually shot anyone, she'd been involved in cases where innocent people were killed or injured. It was a painful reality of law enforcement.

He gave a quick nod. "The important thing now is to get the son of a bitch responsible for shooting Jess."

"Aiming at you," she said. "I've had all night to think about why somebody wants to kill you. Want to hear what I've come up with?"

"Give it to me."

"I was sent to the safe house, undercover, to offer you a bribe and find out if you were a dirty cop. Which you aren't." She offered a tentative smile that he didn't return. "But somebody else is—a Denver cop who is likely on the payroll of Nicholas Dirk. When you started poking around in Dirk's business, you became a threat."

"Why?"

"Think about it," she said. "You're in a unique position. You're familiar with the cops in Denver which means you might have evidence that you're not even aware of. Also, you've lived in this area and know the people here. If you start investigating, you might be the one person who could put all the pieces together."

Abby paused and took a breath. There was something else she needed to say. "I'm pretty sure Leo Fisher is involved with this."

"The undercover FBI agent who was at the drug sting."

She nodded. "The guy you shot in the leg. He's investigating on his own."

"How do you know this?"

"I talked to him." Her forehead tightened in a frown. Telling the whole truth wasn't easy. "Leo and I used to be engaged."

He blinked. "I shot your former fiancé?"

"Not a problem for me," she said quickly. "What happens to Leo is no longer my concern."

"So you don't care that I shot him," Mac said. "Must have been a really bad breakup."

She had no intention of giving out details

on that humiliating experience. "You might say so."

Slowly, Mac nodded. "So you're a part of this, too. You're connected to Leo."

"Technically? No. We're not on the same case. Leo was undercover with the drug dealers. My assignment was you. And that assignment is over. If I follow procedure, I'll file my report and move on."

Thus far, she hadn't actually lied to her supervisor; she just hadn't filed the report stating the result of her attempted bribe. Quite easily, she could pretend that she needed to stay with the investigation so she could keep an eye on Mac.

If she leveled with her supervisor and told him that she wanted to stay and help Mac, she knew the answer. A resounding negative. Mac's proposed investigation went far outside the boundary of accepted law enforcement procedure. He was looking for revenge. Following that path led to rogue behavior. It was dangerous.

He reached out and took her hand in his. "Don't leave, Abby. I need you."

When she gazed into his cool blue eyes, she recognized a depth of honesty and sincerity that touched her soul. He was a good man. And he had been terribly wronged, suspected by the very people who should have respected him. "If we work together, you'll have to trust me. Can you do that?"

"Not a bit." A slow, sexy grin spread across his face. "That's what makes this interesting."

Very interesting. "Why do you think you need me?"

"This investigation will require undercover skills," he said. "That's not my thing."

She nodded in vigorous agreement. "You're the worst liar I've ever seen. I mean, it's pathetic, Mac."

"Right."

His annoyance was obvious in his voice, and she couldn't stop herself from teasing him. "It's like you're hooked up to a permanent lie detector."

"I get the picture."

"Grade school kids lying about how the dog ate their homework do better than you."

"Enough." He squeezed her hand. "You're going to have to show me how to go undercover. I need to get close to Dirk and to talk to the cops back in Denver without letting them know what I'm doing."

"Where do we start?"

"There's a party tomorrow night at Dirk's house. Have you seen that place? It's massive."

"I know," she said. "I followed you and Jess when you drove by."

"How did you do that? How did you track us to the rapids?"

"Easy," she said smugly. "I planted a homing device in your boot and used my handy-dandy GPS locator to pinpoint your location."

His grip on her hand tightened. "You were spying on me."

"Damn right." She squeezed back, hard enough that he noticed. "It's a good thing that I was. If I hadn't showed up at the rapids when I did…"

She left the sentence hanging. Neither of them needed to be reminded about Jess.

Mac lifted her hand to his lips and brushed a light kiss across her knuckles. "Did I ever thank you for saving my life?"

"Actually, no." His unexpected tenderness caused her heart to skip a beat. "When we got to the hospital, you were totally obnoxious. However, you did say that I was pretty."

"That's true," he said.

"It's time to leave truth behind and start up a cover story."

She reclaimed her hand and hopped off the bed. Being close to him made thinking difficult, and she couldn't afford to make any mistakes in this admittedly rogue assignment. "The best lies come from sticking to what you know. So, here's your cover story. After the incident at the warehouse, you realized that you're sick and tired of Denver and thinking of moving back to the mountains."

"That's it?"

"Simple," she said. "And I'm your recent girlfriend, somebody you met at a lodge. I'll be Abby."

"Not Vanessa the former Vegas showgirl?"

"Only when we're at the safe house. Maybe not even then." She frowned. "I guarantee that Julia is not going to be happy about our plans."

When Mac and Abby returned to the safe house that afternoon, they didn't have to look far to find Julia Last. She was out by the stables, chopping wood. Her long brown ponytail flipped behind her as she weilded her axe, splitting logs into fireplace-sized chunks.

Her strength and skill were impressive. Mac liked this sturdy, capable woman. He hoped that he and Abby wouldn't have to lie to Julia.

Bending down, he picked up one of the logs she'd split and placed it on the growing wood pile. "Hard work."

"It keeps me in shape," she said. "I heard what happened to your friend. I'm real sorry."

"Jess is going to pull through." Before they left the hospital, Mac had stopped in to see Jess. He was barely conscious and still being closely monitored. He couldn't remember anything about what hap-pened at the rapids which, Mac thought, was fortunate. He wished he could forget that moment of stark terror when he realized the rifleman was aiming at them…at Jess.

"These mountain men," Abby said, "are tough."

"Must be," Julia said. Though the afternoon was cool, she wore a short-sleeved T-shirt. Across her ample bosom was a logo that read: She Who Laughs…Lasts. Reaching up, she wiped her fore-head with the back of her hand. "I heard it was a hunting accident."

"That's not exactly what happened," Abby said.

Though Abby was physically much smaller than Julia, Mac saw a similarity between the two woman. Both were well-trained federal agents. They both carried themselves with confidence. Now that Abby had dropped the sex-bomb act, her gaze was steady and measured. A lot was going on behind her dark brown eyes.

"I don't want to know details," Julia said.

"Understood," Mac said. "And we don't want to get you in trouble."

"Which is exactly why I don't want to know anything more about this supposed hunting accident. If I had to guess, though…" Her unflappable gaze scanned his face. "…I might think that your friend was shot by mistake. I might guess that you, Mac, were the real target."

He gave a quick nod.

Julia placed another piece of wood on the cutting block, then turned to Abby. "You're not exactly in character, Vanessa Nye. If I were inclined to make another wild guess, I might assume that you and Mac are working together now."

Abby started, "Julia, I—"

"Don't want to know." She raised the axe over her head and split the log with one whack. "If someone is gunning for Mac—not that I have any reason to believe that's true—it's a good thing that you're both staying here. Because this is a safe house. Our perimeters are monitored. We're well-armed. While you're here, you're very, very safe."

Before Julia could lift the axe again, Abby hugged her. "Thank you."

Julia held her at arm's length and grinned. "I like seeing you two together. From the first minute you met, there were sparks."

"Not really," Abby said.

Silently, Mac echoed Abby's doubts. Though he'd had an immediate appreciation of her well-displayed cleavage when they first met, he had suspected her motives. Vanessa Nye was a personification of all the manipulative women he'd ever known.

"Definite sparks," Julia repeated. "Not that I'm a matchmaker. And this safe house isn't the FBI version of the Dating Game. But I like to see a little romance. Especially for you, Abby. Being a female agent can be rough on relationships."

Relationships? Mac didn't like the sound of that word. What the hell were they talking about?

A wry smile crooked the corner of Abby's mouth. "I don't know about sparks and romance, but you're right about relationships, Julia. Being undercover means you have too many secrets to keep."

"An agent has too many rules to follow," Julia said.

"Too many responsibilities," Abby added.

Mac wasn't following the focus of their conversation. It was like one of those talk shows where women burst into tears or applauded for no apparent reason.

"At the end of the day," Julia said, "a female agent has nobody to talk to."

"It gets lonely," Abby said.

Julia's gaze encompassed Mac. "Take care of each other. I'll give you until the end of the weekend to get this mess straightened out. Monday morning is when I file my reports."

"What about Roger and the other people

who are staying here?" Mac asked. "Do we need to tell them anything?"

"The other agents work for me. I'm senior. They do what I tell them." She hefted her axe. "But it might be best if you take your meals in your room and limit contact with the others."

As she returned to her chores, Mac and Abby walked back toward the house. In a low voice, he asked, "What just happened?"

"Julia's on our side. She's giving us implied permission to follow our own investigation."

"Why do we need her blessing?"

"Number one," Abby said, "because we can stay here where it's safe."

That much he understood. Paul had wanted Mac to come home with him—a friendly offer that could have put his family in jeopardy. "What's number two?"

"By working with you, I'm breaking the rules. Julia isn't going to blow the whistle. Not until Monday."

"Could you get fired?"

"Oh, yeah."

Mac paused on the deck outside the kitchen door. Until now, he hadn't seen the situation from Abby's perspective. By working with him, she was risking her career. "If you want to back off, I'll understand."

"Let's go up to my room." She pushed open the kitchen door and made a beeline for the staircase leading up to her bedroom. Inside, she closed the door behind him.

"Abby, you didn't answer me."

She sat on the edge of her bed. Now that she was acting like herself, her movements were precise and self-assured. Even her platinum blond hair seemed less artificial. It was as if she knew what she wanted and didn't have patience with wasted action. When she removed her high-heeled boots, this simple action was as graceful as a choreographed dance.

He tore his gaze away from the well-shaped arch of her foot. "I don't want you to lose your job because of me."

"You need me, Mac. You said it yourself. There's no way you can pull off an undercover investigation without my expertise. And I've made a decision to help you."

"Why?"

She hopped off the bed and knelt beside it. Her arms reached under the bed to pull out a suitcase. "Sometimes, the judgments we make in law enforcement are unfair. More than that, they're just plain wrong. I don't like what happened to you. You didn't deserve to be under suspicion. And you certainly didn't deserve to be shot at. What happened to Jess was wrong."

"And you want to make it right."

"I wish I could." When she looked up at him, he saw honest concern in her expression. Her irises were so dark they seemed almost black. "I wish I could wave a magic wand and turn back time. But I can't. Helping you is the next best thing."

"Are you sure?"

"I am for now. Don't push it." She placed the suitcase on top of her bed and flipped it open. "Tools of the trade."

He looked down at the contents of her suitcase. Of course, he was familiar with the workings of her Glock automatic pistols and holsters. Also, he'd seen some of the bugging devices. But there were lots of other gadgets. "Cool stuff. Where's the thing you planted in my boot to track me?"

She opened a smaller case to display an array of tiny flat pieces of plastic. She held the smallest in her manicured fingers. "This transmits a homing signal. Simple micro-technology." She pointed to a shiny disk. "This one is a miniature camera for surveillance."

He picked up a pair of sparkly earrings. "And these?"

"It's a walkie-talkie, capable of audio communication within half a mile range." She took the earrings from him and playfully held them to his ears. "I don't think these would work for you."

"Not unless I was undercover as my great-aunt Lucille MacCloud."

"Hah! You wouldn't make a good woman. Not with that nose."

"What's wrong with it?" He massaged the bridge of his nose. "I've seen worse."

"It's not a bad nose. Just too manly. All your features are masculine. The Adam's apple. The deep-set eyes. The heavy brow. Your ears are too big." She dropped the earrings and held his face in her hands, assessing his features. "I suppose a wig would disguise the ears."

"A wig?"

Teasing, her thumb brushed his mouth. "A

little lipstick. A peach tone, I think." She stroked his eyebrows. "And these would have to be plucked. Maybe shaved."

"Not in this lifetime." Mac had a whole lot of reasons why he wouldn't pass as a female—most obvious was the sudden heat he felt in his groin when Abby began touching him. He hadn't forgotten their moments of sexuality. Their kisses. They'd shared a couple of great kisses for all the wrong reasons.

His mind lingered on those moments, and he realized how much he wanted to kiss her now that he knew her true identity. Julia's words repeated themselves in his head: *This safe house isn't the FBI version of the* Dating Game.

Mac looked away from Abby's tempting lips. "Have you ever gone undercover as a man?"

"Once," she said. "In Jerusalem."

"I didn't think the FBI operated abroad."

"Of course, we don't." She picked up a metallic pen. "This is a single shot weapon. Not very effective except at extreme close range."

"But really a great toy." Glad for the distraction, Mac took the pen from her and balanced it between his fingers. "Do you use all this stuff?"

"I try not to. If I have to resort to weaponry, it usually means my assignment has gone wrong. My job is to gather information."

Though he appreciated her professional attitude, this cool display of competence was a hundred times more seductive than all her prancing around as Vanessa Nye. It was becoming difficult for him to concentrate on the topic at hand. He wanted to caress her shoulders, to gather her slender body in his arms and make love to her.

They were safe here. Julia had promised they'd be safe. He could spend the night here, in Abby's bed. They could—

"Mac!" She snapped her fingers in front of his eyes. "Pay attention."

He nodded.

"My kind of investigating is a lot different than yours. I avoid confrontation and seldom make an arrest. Sometimes, there's a sting and I'm involved. Usually, I pass on the information and get out of the way."

"Not this time," he said.

"What do you mean?"

"If I find the guy responsible for shooting Jess, I'm not going to sit back and wait for somebody else to bust him."

Her eyes flashed. "This isn't a revenge mission."

"Maybe not for you."

Chapter Nine

Abby studied him carefully. Though she understood Mac's desire for vengeance, she couldn't condone it. She needed to clarify their goals before they went any further. "I won't participate in a vendetta. We have two objectives. Identify the dishonest cops. And find the person who wants to kill you."

"And the bastard who shot Jess."

"We follow procedures. Arrests will be made."

"Right," he said. "It's not my plan to charge in with guns blazing like the showdown at the OK Corral. But I will see justice done. The shooter and the guy who sent him will pay for their crime."

"Spoken like a cop."

"That's who I am."

She needed to be sure they were on the same

page, that he wasn't going to take the law into his own hands. "Can I trust you, Mac?"

"That's funny, coming from you."

"Give me your word that you'll follow procedure. If it's necessary for someone else to make the arrest, so be it."

Reluctantly, he held out his hand. "Shake on it."

His fingers gripped her hand with a firm strength. When she looked into his eyes, she saw no hint of deception. But there was a spark. A definite spark.

Their hands remained clasped, and she felt a strong pull that was almost magnetic, drawing her closer to him. She'd been embarrassed when Julia talked about a possible relationship, but she couldn't deny these feelings.

Not again. Not with a cop. Abby dropped his hand and took a step back. She didn't want to think that she was joining with Mac because of her attraction to him—even though her pulse rate doubled every time he touched her. This was business. Law enforcement business.

She closed the suitcase but left it on the bed beside her, creating a barrier between her and Mac. Her attitude must be strictly professional. "We'll have time later to check equipment. The first part of undercover work is teaching you how to lie."

He dug into the pocket of his jeans and pulled out his cell phone. "I know just where to start. There's a message on here to call my partner in Denver. Sheila."

Abby recalled the meeting she observed between Mac and Sheila at the graveyard. "Have you spoken to her about your suspicions?"

"I asked her to look into Nicholas Dirk," Mac admitted. "She talked to Vince Elliot. He's a vice cop. And he told her that I should back off."

"Vince Elliot was also at the warehouse shooting."

"Right."

"He might be the one on Dirk's payroll," she said. "Let's connect the dots. You talk to Sheila. She talks to Vince about Dirk. Then, somebody tries to kill you. I'd have to say, at this point, Vince Elliot is a most suspicious person."

Mac sat on the bed on the other side of her suitcase. He leaned back on his elbows, and his long legs stretched out in front of him. "What about Leo Fisher?"

"He's not taking bribes," she said. "But he's a problem. If he's deeply undercover, getting cozy with Dirk, he wouldn't mind sacrificing you."

"Even though I'm a cop?"

"Leo is kind of intense. When he's on a case, he forgets scruples."

"And you were engaged to this jerk?"

She pointed to his phone. "Call Sheila. Tell her your cover story about being sick and tired of police work and thinking about moving back home to the mountains."

"She's going to ask about the shooting," Mac said.

"Claim amnesia. Tell her that you can't remember what happened until you woke up in the hospital."

She watched him make the call, observing his technique. His voice faltered slightly on the word "amnesia," and he added an unnecessary embellishment about seeing somebody dressed like a hunter. Other than that, he sounded like he was telling the truth.

The problem was in his facial expressions and his body language. With every lie, his expression altered. His gaze flicked upward as if he was searching for a falsehood. He blinked repeatedly. His fists clenched, then he rubbed at his mouth and the side of his nose—classic signs of lying.

When he talked to Sheila about his new girlfriend named Abby, he gave her a sheepish, uncomfortable grin that was so out of character for cynical Mac that she almost laughed out loud.

He disconnected the call and turned to her. "How did I do?"

"Your voice wasn't bad," she said. "The tone was steady except for a couple of times. Keep in mind that when you're building an undercover identity, it's best to say as little as possible."

"This isn't an undercover identity," he objected.

"But it is. You're pretending to be a different Mac Granger—an unsuspicious guy who hates his job as a big city cop."

He scoffed. "Nobody who knows me will believe that."

"Not unless you give them a reason why you've changed," she said. "You need to pretend that you love being back home in the mountains, that there's no place on earth you'd rather be."

"That's a hell of a stretch."

She was curious about his reasons for not liking this spectacular country, but this was not the time for analysis. He needed a crash course in lying. "Use your imagination. Think about the positives. What do you like about being in the mountains?"

"Friends," he said. "It's good to be around Jess and Paul."

"What else?"

"I can't hate the natural beauty of the mountains in fall. The turning aspens. The endless blue sky." His gaze lifted as if he could see through the ceiling, then he focused very directly upon her. "And then, there's you. According to this cover story, you're supposed to be my girlfriend. I'm supposed to be falling in love with you, right?"

"That's the story."

"That might be more believable, if it was more true." He rose from the bed and took one step to stand in front of her. "Both times when we kissed, it was a lie. I was trying to force your hand."

"And I was playing the part of Vanessa." Her breath caught in her throat. She knew what was coming next.

He took her hands and pulled her to her feet. "Kiss me now. As yourself."

"That might not be wise." Even as she spoke, she knew resistance was futile. With every fiber of her being, she wanted to kiss him.

"Kiss me, Abigail Nelson."

She melted into his arms. When their lips met, it was different from their other kisses. Instead of fierce and demanding, he was oh-so-gentle. His approach was sweet and cajoling, subtly urging her to drop all barriers and come closer.

Her arm encircled his torso. Their bodies skimmed against each other. His fingertips lightly caressed her back and shoulders, teasing her budding excitement into full flower. Her stomach began to flutter. Sensation built gradually, slowly. Oh yes, this kiss was very different.

Before, Mac had overwhelmed her. Now, she could feel respect in the way he held her. He was a gentleman, making a promise. In his arms, she knew she would be well loved and thoroughly satisfied.

When he ended their kiss and gazed down into her eyes, she struggled to be professional. "Very convincing. If I didn't know better, I'd think I was your girlfriend."

"But you still have doubts," he said. "I can do better."

"By all means, try again."

She surrendered to his embrace. Their bodies molded together so tightly that she could feel the breath in his lungs and the rhythm of his heartbeat. Her legs separated, and she felt his hard arousal. Slowly, she ground her hips against him.

A moan rumbled in the back of his throat. He deepened the kiss. His tongue engaged with hers.

When his hand glided up her torso and touched the edge of her breast, an exquisite thrill raced through her.

All of her FBI training warned her that this intimacy was a huge mistake. It was bad enough that she'd abandoned her assignment. She shouldn't lose all semblance of professional detachment by making love to the man she was supposed to investigate.

But Abby didn't care. She wanted him in the most intimate way that a woman wants a man. She'd already broken the rules. Why not go all the way?

She leaned backward, pulling him down onto the bed on top of her. Her suitcase of surveillance and espionage tools rubbed against her hip, reminding her of their real reason for being together.

He gazed down at her. An amazing glow emanated from his blue eyes. "Is this what you want?"

Here was her chance to object, to end this seduction before it went too far. But that wasn't her decision. Her voice was breathless as she whispered, "Make love to me, Mac."

With a sweep of his arm, he shoved the suitcase off the bed. He tore back the down comforter on her bed. Amid kisses and caresses, their clothing peeled away. Very quickly, they were naked in each other's arms.

Mac showed no sign of hesitation, though his body was bruised and the stitches on his shoulder were still bandaged. He was clearly the one in control. His every touch, taste and whisper aroused her even more, and she abandoned herself to his amazingly considerate maneuvers.

When he nuzzled the base of her throat, she gasped with pleasure and said, "You've done this before."

"Once or twice."

"You're really good at it."

Propped on his elbows above her, he stroked her cheek. "You inspire me, Abby."

She arched her back, rubbing against his erection. "You know I'm not really a blonde."

"I wouldn't care if your hair was purple."

"Well, of course, you would. I don't think you'd—"

He silenced her with another intense kiss that took her breath away. There would be no more teasing on this pathway toward fulfillment. Their rising passion turned serious, and she knew that his lovemaking would change her in ways she had never thought possible.

Until now, her career had been her entire focus. She'd put aside thoughts of one day having a family. As a special agent, constantly traveling and in jeopardy, she couldn't have children. Couldn't have a home. Not a relationship. Not a chance. She'd ignored the emptiness Julia had spoken of.

Oh God, she wanted her life to be different. She longed for the myriad satisfactions a real relationship could give her. A relationship with a man like Mac.

He gently parted her thighs.

She was ready for him. Hot. Wet. She wanted this.

Sheathed in a condom, he entered her slowly. Inch by inch, he filled her. Her muscles clenched tightly around his manhood. Slowly, he withdrew, then thrust again, harder and deeper, again and again. Her heart beat so fast that she thought it would surely explode. Wild shudders shot through her body from her scalp to her toenails, and she abandoned herself to this unbelievable climax.

Though it was still daylight outside the windows of her bedroom, she saw stars. And planets. She saw the entire universe in his eyes.

He collapsed on the bed beside her, and she nestled in his arms. This was bliss. Complete bliss.

"I think," Mac said, "I can convince people that you're my girlfriend."

"Really?"

"It wouldn't be a lie, Abby."

Chapter Ten

The next day, Mac's head was spinning with all Abby's instructions on how to be a liar. As a homicide detective, he'd conducted hundreds, maybe thousands, of interrogations. He knew the techniques, knew how to spot when someone else was lying.

Even though he knew *how* to lie, he just couldn't do it. Somehow, he had to control the involuntary flicking of his eyes and the tendency to touch his face. *But those tics were involuntary!* He had no control over them. It wasn't his fault that he was an intrinsically honest man.

Abby had suggested alternate physical cues for when he was about to deviate from the truth. He should make a conscious effort to substitute another behavior for his natural reaction. They'd tried a laugh which came out sounding moronic. People wouldn't think he was lying…just that he was the village idiot. Then he did a tapping on his thigh. Also clumsy. Finally, they'd settled on clearing his throat and giving a slow blink.

As they left the safe house and headed to his car, Abby said, "Give it a try. Tell me a lie."

"About what?"

"Anything. Tell me the blue sky is red. Tell me you hate broccoli."

"I *do* hate broccoli."

"Lie to me, Mac."

If she'd been a classroom instructor, this was the point at which he would walk out of the room in annoyance. But she was Abby. She had come to mean something special to him.

He gazed down at the woman who strode confidently beside him. Her Vanessa persona was gone. Though she still had the platinum blond hair, it fell straight to her shoulders, framing her lovely face. She seemed to grow more beautiful with every hour he passed in her company. An amazing phenomenon. One that he deeply appreciated.

He felt a warm grin spread across his face. They hadn't occupied all their time last night with his training. There had been hours of passion.

Abby was an amazing lover—compliant but not docile. Her body had responded to his touch with an eagerness that encouraged him. And she had been inventive. Last night in the shower, she had treated him to a delicate, sensual, full-body wash worthy of a geisha.

Today, he wanted to show her how much she meant to him. He paused at the driver's side door of his car and tried to come up with a lie. This should be something big and important, not just a casual reference to the color of the sky.

He cleared his throat. Slowly, he blinked, preparing himself for the greatest lie he'd ever told. "My mother, Katherine MacCloud Granger, was a trustworthy woman. From her example, I learned that all women are to be taken at their word."

Abby's eyebrows raised. It was obvious that she hadn't expected this statement. "Was there an event that convinced you that your mother was above reproach?"

He cleared his throat again, not wanting to continue. This incident from his youth formed the central core to his belief system. It was not to be taken lightly.

He lied, "For one thing, she never cheated on my father. And if she did, I never found out about it. I never had to sit across the dining room table, watching her smile at my dad and serve his favorite foods while I knew she was unfaithful. I never saw her disloyalty."

The lies failed him, and he spoke the truth. "I learned the hard way. I couldn't trust her. My own mother."

Abby threw her arms around him. "I'm so sorry."

Never before had Mac made this declaration aloud. He hadn't told his father or his friends or the Denver P.D. shrink. Putting the words out there gave him a measure of relief. As he held Abby, he felt a knot around his heart loosen. "How did I do?"

"You're not a great liar." She glanced up at him. "But you're a very good man, and I hope to win your trust. Is that possible?"

Not likely. There was a lot to admire about Abby Nelson, but her job was undercover deception. When it came to lying, she was an expert. He'd be a fool to think she would always tell the truth. His expression must have provided her with the answer to her question because she gave him a sad smile and stepped out of his embrace.

"There's something we need to keep in mind today," she said. "Somebody tried to kill you at the rapids. That could very well happen again."

"Especially at Dirk's party tonight."

That event loomed before them. If, in fact, Nicholas Dirk was high up the ladder in drug distribution, he was a dangerous man—a man who might have ordered Mac killed, a man who might have bribed Denver cops. Getting close to Dirk was the thread that might unravel all these complications.

But first, they were going to the hospital to visit Jess. Mac got behind the steering wheel and fired up the engine.

"We should get flowers for Jess," Abby said.

"I suppose so." It would take a lot more than a bouquet to quell his rage and guilt about Jess's wounds. Jess was in the hospital because Mac had been investigating where he had no business to be concerned. And now he was planning to dig deeper. Was this another mistake? One that would have even more disastrous consequences?

BEFORE ABBY entered Jess's hospital room, she smelled a heavy floral perfume, totally inappropriate for a hospital. Then, she saw the cause: his room was a kaleidoscope of color. Every flat surface—including the other unoccupied bed—held get-well bouquets. She glanced down at the handful of daisies they'd bought at the hospital shop. No wonder there hadn't been much of a selection.

While she tucked their daisies into the array, Mac went directly to his friend's bedside. "I see the flowers. Where are the girls who sent them?"

Weakly, Jess opened his eyes. "Had to go. I need sleep."

Abby noted the IV drip, the monitors and the button at Jess's fingertips. He had to be in pain and heavily sedated. It had only been two days since he'd taken a bullet in the chest.

Even so, he managed to look handsome in a pale, exhausted way. Some guys were destined to be gorgeous no matter what. She came up beside the bed and patted his hand. "You're tired. We won't stay too long."

Jess cocked his head to study her. "Vanessa?"

"Actually," Mac said, "her name is Abby. Nothing for you to worry about. We've got it all sorted out."

"I can see." A feeble smile curved his mouth. "You're a couple. That's good. You need a woman, Mac."

"That's your solution to everything. Grab a girl."

Though Mac's words were teasing, there was a note of fondness in his voice that touched Abby's heart. Even though these men hadn't spent a lot of time together in recent years, the bond between them was solid.

Jess frowned. "What happened, Mac? How did I get shot? I still don't remember."

She heard Mac clear his throat, preparing to lie. It was a necessary deception. If Jess recalled, he might be in danger.

"A hunting accident," Mac said. "Some jerk got careless. I didn't even see him."

Apparently satisfied, Jess nodded. He leaned back against the pillows and closed his eyes. "A lot of idiots out there during hunting season. I warned you."

"And I should have listened," Mac said.

"It's a bummer." His voice was fading. "I'm going to miss the first day of skiing."

Mac cradled his friend's limp hand. When he cleared his throat this time, it wasn't to lie. Mac was holding back tears. "I'm going to make this right."

"Deep powder snow. I love the powder. Got new ski boots." His eyelids fluttered open. "Hey, Mac. There's somebody here you'll want to talk to. Lisa."

"Lisa Hammond?"

"She's been waiting for me. Tell her to go home. Got to sleep. Now."

As Jess slipped into a dream, Mac stepped away from his bedside and looked at Abby. "Lisa was a girl I dated in high school. She had a kid with Nicholas Dirk."

"Talk to her. She might have inside information about Dirk."

Together, they went down the hospital corridor to a waiting area. Lisa and two other extremely attractive women were waiting. They leaped to their feet and surged around Mac, demanding news about Jess.

"He's sleeping," Mac said. "He wanted me

to tell you to come back tomorrow when he's feeling stronger."

After they exchanged assurances that Jess would recover and it was good to see Mac, only Lisa was left. Abby made an excuse and ducked around a corner to listen while Mac tried out his lying techniques.

He said, "Jess told me you'd been waiting."

"I really wanted to talk to him." Her voice was babyish and soft.

"About what?"

"To be real honest, I'd heard you were in town. I thought we could, like, you know, get together or something."

Lurking around the corner, Abby stuck out her tongue. It sounded like Lisa was, *like, you know,* throwing herself at Mac.

"Tell me about yourself," Mac said. "I hear you have a child. A daughter."

"She's two. Such a little honey. She looks just like me. I named her Heather."

"Pretty name," Mac said. "And the father is Nicholas Dirk."

"You've been asking about me." She giggled. "You miss me, don't you?"

Abby heard Mac clear his throat. "Actually, I'm involved with somebody else right now. I have a girlfriend."

"Is it serious?" Lisa asked.

"Very," Mac said. "Being with her has changed my life."

Though Abby knew Mac was only sticking to their cover story, his declaration pleased her. He almost sounded sincere.

Mac continued, "I'm concerned about you and the father of your child. I don't want to see you hurt, Lisa. And I heard that Nicholas Dirk was into drugs."

"Illegal drugs?"

"You can tell me," Mac said. "Tell me all about Nicholas Dirk."

"Drop dead," Lisa said. "I mean, like, Nick's a jerk for not marrying me. But he's done right by me and Heather. Financially. And he's not a criminal."

"Are you sure?"

"You haven't changed a bit. Still Mister Righteous. You and Paul and Jess. You're like, the Righteous Friends."

"Lisa, I'm—"

"Forget it."

Abby heard Lisa's footsteps marching away from Mac. Could he have possibly handled that conversation worse? The man had a lot to learn about maintaining an undercover identity, and no time to learn the techniques.

Abby had her work cut out for her.

After visiting hours were over at five o'clock, they left the hospital and went into Vail to shop at the boutiques. She hoped that buying him new clothes would help establish his new identity.

As he parked his car, he said, "I didn't do so bad when I was talking to Lisa. She didn't suspect anything."

"Only because she's dumb as a bump on a stump," Abby said bluntly. "I can't believe you dated her."

"I was young." The way Mac remembered, Lisa had been hot, ripe and willing to be plucked. Apparently, she hadn't changed much. "What was I supposed to say to get information?"

"Always let the subject do the talking. Show yourself to be a willing listener and let them reveal themselves."

Irritated with himself, Mac nodded. He knew these techniques. As a homicide detective, he knew when to threaten, when to push and when to back off. Letting the suspect talk was a basic procedure in the interrogation room—a place where he was clearly in control. But now?

Undercover work was more like socializing. And he'd never been good at small talk.

As they walked away from the underground parking, Mac glanced back over his shoulder. Ever since they'd left the hospital, he sensed they were being followed. There was a car that had stayed behind them almost all the way into the village.

At this time of day, the shadows grew long. The air felt heavy and ominous. *Somebody wanted to kill him.* He needed to be alert, to maintain extreme vigilance.

And yet, when Abby hooked her arm through his and rubbed against him, his irritation faded. He was happier than he had any right to be. As they entered the winding village streets, he heard the cheerful oom-pah-pah of the Oktoberfest tuba. He couldn't help grinning.

She paused outside the polished windows of a small boutique and studied the well-dressed mannequins. "I can't wait to get you into some decent clothes."

"I dress okay."

"For a cop," she said. "But, in a little while, we'll be going to a classy party at Nicholas Dirk's mansion. You want to fit in."

"As what?"

"Think of the cover story," she reminded him. "You're supposed to be a full-time mountain guy."

"A guy who shops at boutiques?" He rolled his eyes. "Did I also become a millionaire?"

"Think about the way Jess dresses. He's not rich, but he always looks great." She gave him a once-over. "We need a silk turtleneck. Pale blue to bring out the color in your eyes."

"You're the expert."

Her own transformation had amazed him. As Vanessa Nye, she'd looked cheap. Now, her smooth hair reminded him of one of those models in the magazines Sheila was always reading. Abby's light makeup allowed her healthy complexion to shine through. Though she still wore leather slacks, her clothes fit better. She looked classy.

He did, however, miss the push-up bra and the cleavage.

In the first shop, they got the turtleneck

and a cashmere scarf in blue and gray. In the second, Mac splurged on a pair of hiking boots—a good investment for winter snow. Plus, his new boots didn't come equipped with the GPS tracking chip she'd planted in his old ones.

Back on the village street, she stared at his crotch. "Your jeans are okay." Her gaze drifted lower. "The bootleg cut is good for hiding your ankle holster."

They were both well-armed. Mac didn't expect to get gunned down on the winding streets of the pseudo-Bavarian village, but it was wise to be prepared. "Could we speed this up? All these people walking around with bratwurst are making me hungry."

"Speed it up?" She arched an eyebrow. "Wishful thinking. You need the perfect jacket."

It took three more boutiques and trying on several different jackets that all felt pretty much the same to him. Finally, Abby gave a satisfied nod. "This is the one."

Dark brown leather and insulated, with a zipper-front, the jacket didn't seem like a big deal until he looked at the price tag. "Are you sure I need this?"

"It'll last forever."

"Which is just about how long I'll be paying for it." He passed his credit card to the clerk. "Are we done now?"

"Not quite." She led him to a full-length mirror. "Take a look at yourself."

Mac seldom bothered with mirrors, except for shaving in the morning. As he checked out his reflection, he had to admit that she'd done a good job. He'd been transformed from big-city cop into mountain chic. "I don't look like me."

"That's the idea." She reached up and stroked his hair. "We should visit a stylist."

"Not necessary." He'd gone to the same barber for the past six years and liked the simplicity of his cut and his hair combed back off his forehead.

"But you have such nice, thick hair."

"No matter how hard you try, I'm not ever going to be as pretty as Jess."

"I like the way you look."

Her voice dropped to a husky register that awakened his desire for her. He slipped his arm around her waist and pulled her close, then checked out the mirror again. Her pale hair shimmered against the dark leather of his jacket. She was exactly the right height for him. The top of her head reached his cheekbone. Exactly the right height for kissing.

The clerk joined them. "You're a handsome couple."

"Thank you," Abby said.

"Meant to be together," the clerk said as he handed over the bag containing Mac's old jacket. "Enjoy the evening."

When they stepped back out onto the street, Mac caught a glimpse of sudden movement in his peripheral vision. He turned his head in time to see a dark figure disappear around the corner. Someone who had been waiting for them to emerge from the shop? He remembered the car that had been following them earlier.

He leaned down to nuzzle Abby's earlobe and spoke quietly, "I have the feeling that we're being tailed."

"Me, too." Her whispered breath was warm on his cheek. "Nothing definite. Just a sense."

"When we go to the parking lot, we'll hang back and wait to see who follows."

"Parking lot? I thought you were hungry."

"I'm not eating lobster tails in Vail when there's a perfectly good Rocky Burger down the road."

They strolled together through the thinning crowd. Most of the Oktoberfest tourists had either gone home or were inside the restaurants and bars. Occasionally, Abby stopped at a window and subtly glanced up and down the street. Mac did the same. Though he saw nothing unusual, the hairs on the back of his neck prickled with apprehension.

When they entered the well-lit underground parking structure, Mac latched on to Abby's hand and pulled her behind a monster-sized Humvee. They ducked down and waited.

Mac drew his gun from the ankle holster. This was one of Abby's weapons, and the heft was different from his own handgun, which he'd had to turn in for ballistics during the I.A. investigation.

Soon, he'd have his weapon back. And his badge, too. With Abby helping him, Mac knew he'd close this case fast.

But now, the minutes ticked slowly by.

Another couple entered and went to their car.

A family came next—mother, father and

two young children whose shouts echoed in the concrete structure.

Then a single figure.

Mac recognized Roger Flannery, the young FBI agent from the safe house.

Chapter Eleven

Mac watched as Roger shuffled halfway down the aisle of cars and climbed into the safe house SUV—a vehicle that was common in the mountains and familiar to both him and Abby. But the SUV hadn't been the car Mac thought was following when they left the hospital. Was there another tail?

He turned to Abby who was crouched beside him. "Let's wait another couple of minutes."

"I can't believe Roger was tailing us."

"Why not? We know somebody in law enforcement has been taking bribes."

"But he's FBI."

She sounded shocked, as if the feds were virgin pure and incapable of corruption. Mac knew better. Dishonesty wasn't limited to the Denver P.D. He'd be relieved to find out that Roger was the guilty party—pretending to be a hapless rookie while he was working for the bad guys.

"Also," Abby whispered, "Roger isn't competent at surveillance. Remember when we ditched him."

"He could be playing us."

"No way." Her vehemence told him that Abby didn't think she could be conned. This was her training, her field of expertise. Supposedly, she could ID another undercover agent in a flash.

They stayed behind the Humvee for another ten minutes. No one but innocent-looking families entered the parking area.

Roger started his engine and exited the structure. As he passed their hiding place, they saw him talking on a cell phone.

When he was gone, Abby stood. "I'm sure there's an explanation for Roger's behavior. I should call Julia."

"What if she's in on it? She's lived up here for a while and might have contact with Dirk." But Mac didn't really believe Julia was involved. "I hate to think badly of her. She seems like a good person."

"A good agent," Abby said. Her cell phone

was in her hand. "If Roger is working with the bad guys, she needs to know."

He closed his hand over hers. "For the moment, let's keep our suspicions about Roger to ourselves."

"Why?"

"So we can see how it fits into the puzzle."

She shoved her cell phone back in her purse. "What's next?"

"Rocky Burgers."

THE LITTLE RESTAURANT near Redding was full, and they had to wait for a booth, which was no problem because they didn't want to arrive at Dirk's party too early.

Though this had been a regular hangout during Mac's high school days, he only saw one other person he knew—a casual acquaintance who immediately asked about Jess and cursed the carelessness of the lamebrained riflemen who flooded the mountains during the hunting seasons.

When their table was ready, Mac took the seat facing the door so he could keep an eye on the Rocky Burger patrons, coming and going. Though he maintained vigilence, his conversation with Abby was casual as though they were on a date. Dating? That thought seemed backwards since they'd already made love.

When this investigation was over, he wondered if they would stay together. A relationship? He shuddered at that word. In his experience, relationships were trouble. Sooner or later, somebody was going to be disappointed.

After they'd finished their burgers and curly fries, it was time for Nicholas's party. Their plan was simple: Play their undercover roles and gather information.

As Mac drove, following the same route that Jess had taken before he was shot, he tried to narrow their focus. "When you fired at the hunter with the rifle, did you hit him?"

"I might have winged him," she said. "Why?"

"I was hoping for an obvious clue, like a limp. Or an arm in a sling."

"If I hit him," she said, "the wound was nothing serious because he took off in a flash. Didn't even return fire."

"He was working alone," Mac concluded.

She flipped down the visor and used the mirror to apply a fresh coat of lipstick. "How do I look?"

"Hot and high class." When she shot him a sexy glance, he almost drove off the two-lane road. "Seductive."

"Let's hope Dirk thinks so. I want to get close to him."

Mac didn't like the idea of other men leering at her beautiful face and sensual curves. "Not too close."

"I can take care of myself."

He checked the rearview mirror as they passed the condo development and took the turn toward the more exclusive properties. The headlights of another car followed. Mac took a detour. The other headlights stayed with him. "We've got a tail."

"They're probably going to the same place we are."

"We'll see." He signaled and pulled onto the shoulder to let the other car pass.

Instead of cruising by, the other car pulled onto the shoulder in front of them. This could be trouble.

Remembering his days as a patrolman, Mac took the gun from his ankle holster. "I'll see what he wants."

"Don't." Abby touched his arm. "If they want you dead, don't give them an easy target."

The driver's side door on the car in front of them opened, and a man stepped out. Mac recognized Vince Elliot.

Still holding his pistol, Mac stepped out of his car. "What's a Denver vice cop doing in the mountains?"

"You know why I'm here."

"Tell me."

"We're both going to the same place. Nicholas Dirk's house."

"Right." But why? Why was Vince associating with Dirk?

Mac heard the passenger side door on his car open. A quick glance showed him that Abby had stepped out. Though he didn't see her weapon, he was certain that she was armed. She kept a careful distance, using the front fender of his vehicle as a shield.

His mind flashed back to the scene at the warehouse. If Sheila had been as smart as Abby, none of this would have happened.

Vince came toward him, keeping his hands out of his pockets. "Go home, Mac. This is an undercover operation. You don't belong here."

"My friend was shot."

"I heard about that. Hunting accident?"

Mac heard Abby clear her throat, reminding him to keep his cover story intact. It didn't feel right to lie to Vince Elliot. They'd been rookies at the same time. Mac had met Vince's long-time girlfriend.

But Vince was on his way to Nicholas's party. He could be the dirty cop.

Mac cleared his throat and blinked. And lied. "Yeah, a hunting accident. It reminded me that life is short. I'm sick of being in the line of fire. Might be time for me to hang it up. Maybe move back to the mountains."

In the glare of the headlights, Mac saw suspicion on Vince's face. "But you love being a cop."

"That was before I got shot." An honest surge of anger gave weight to his next words. "You remember what happened at the warehouse. Don't you, Vince? I stepped in front of you and took a bullet."

"Doing your job."

And what had Mac's efforts gotten him? Unfounded suspicions. An enforced recuperation at a safe house where Abby was supposed to bribe him. "When you talked to Internal Affairs, did you stand up for me?"

"I couldn't see what happened. I was facedown on the pavement. It happened too fast."

Not in Mac's memory. Every second before the fatal shooting had felt like an hour. "Next time, you might want to keep your eyes open. It's a good way to spot your allies. And your enemies."

Vince shrugged. "Are you really thinking about retirement?"

"Thinking about it." Mac cleared his throat and nodded toward Abby. "This lady is making me think seriously about it."

He introduced Abby and Vince. Neither of them moved closer to each other.

When Vince turned to him again, his features were arranged in a amiable expression. "How can you afford to retire? Did you come into a family fortune?"

Mac recognized the probe. Vince was indirectly asking if he'd taken a payoff, a bribe. *Bastard!* It took all Mac's willpower not to slap that fake congeniality off Vince's face. *Lying bastard!*

Abby piped up, "Mac can find a better job. Cops don't earn that much money."

"Overworked and underpaid." Vince's

grin didn't reach his eyes. "Have you got a line on another job, Mac?"

"Developer," Abby said. "I've been wanting to invest up here. To put my inheritance to work. Mac can help me. He could become a developer. That's what Nicholas Dirk does, right?"

Vince turned toward her. "Right."

"That's why we're going to this party," Abby said.

Mac couldn't help being impressed by how quickly she'd knitted together a simple cover story. The woman was a brilliant liar. Her talents put Vince's vice cop abilities to shame.

Mac turned to Vince. "How do you know Dirk?"

"Friend of a friend." Vince took a step back. Apparently, he knew when he'd been bested. "See you there."

"Wait!" Mac closed the space between them. "Earlier you said something about an undercover operation."

"Did I?"

"Oh, yeah. You said I didn't belong here." Thanks to Abby's cover story, the tables had turned. Vince was now on the defensive. "Tell me the truth, Vince."

"Just watch your step." He glanced toward Abby. "Both of you."

Vince pivoted, returned to his car and drove off.

Behind the wheel of his car, Mac let out a triumphant whoop. He grabbed Abby and kissed her. "You're a genius!"

"I'm good," she said. "Very good."

"I wish I had a camera on Vince, that lying bastard. Did you see how his face collapsed when you gave him a good reason why we wanted to meet Dirk?"

"I saw," Abby said.

She snuggled up against Mac and lightly stroked his chin. His stubble had begun to grow out, and she liked the rasping sensation against her fingertips.

Again, he gave her a big smack on the lips. "How'd you come up with that story about the inheritance and becoming a developer?"

"Wishful thinking. I always wanted to be an heiress." And, if this investigation didn't turn out well, she might need another source of income. "I remembered that lie you told about your family owning the land Vail was built on."

"You knew I was lying?"

"Oh, yeah."

"But you kissed me, anyway."

"A girl's got to do what a girl's got to do." She pulled away from him and pulled down the visor mirror again. "I need to fix my lipstick. No more kissing."

He started the car and drove the rest of the way to Nicholas Dirk's chalet where a long line of parked cars stretched along the side of the road. The heavy iron gates at the entryway stood open, but there were two muscular guys standing watch. Even if they weren't searched before entering, Abby figured those guys would notice the bulge of a concealed weapon. "Take off your ankle holster, Mac."

She stowed her own handgun in the glove compartment.

He unfastened the ankle holster. "I'm keeping this cool one-bullet pen in my pocket."

She was also subtly armed. Her silver bracelet held a swichblade, and her karate skills were outstanding. She wasn't afraid. The opposite, in fact. Stepping into a dangerous situation with only her wits to protect her gave her a buzz.

Before leaving the car, she warned, "We

have to assume that the security at this place is extensive."

"That's what Jess told me."

She envisioned listening devices the size of pinpoints and the unblinking eyes of tiny cameras. "Once we're inside, we'll be under constant observation. Be careful what you say."

Though she'd done this type of operation many times before, Abby usually worked alone. She didn't know what to expect from Mac when it came to peeling back this many layers of deception.

When they were stopped at the gate, Mac identified himself and added, "I'm a friend of Jess Isler."

One of the husky young men looked angry. "I heard what happened to Jess. Damn hunters!"

"He's going to be okay. Doesn't even remember what happened."

"Hey, aren't you the guy who was with Jess when he got shot?"

"That's right. We were at the rapids." Mac cleared his throat and blinked slowly. "I heard the bang, then I fell off the rocks into the creek. When I whacked my head on a boulder, I got all the memory knocked out of me. Want to feel the bump?"

Abby stood beside him, smiling. Mac was doing well. In one simple lie, he had defused any fears these guards might have about being identified if, in fact, one of them was the shooter.

Hand-in-hand, they strolled up the wide, well-lit driveway to the entrance of the towering chateau. The southern side was a wall of windows, and they could see the crowd of partygoers. Their conversation and giddy laughter harmonized with the plaintive wail of a live jazz quartet.

Inside a three-story entryway was a coat check. The catered buffet and open bar underscored the casual but costly tone of a mountain party in Vail.

Abby was glad she'd forced Mac to dress upscale. In his silk turtleneck and pricey hiking boots, he fit right in...perhaps even more than she did. Whether Mac liked it or not, he was accepted as a local. Several people approached him to ask about Jess and to tell Mac that it was time he moved back here where he belonged.

In the swirl of introductions, she almost

didn't notice Leo. Drink in hand, he leaned an elbow on the baby grand piano, posing with his silver-headed cane. His gaze met hers, then he quickly looked away. A cold shiver slid down her backbone. Leo Fisher was here. *And* Vince Elliot, the vice cop. The undercover operatives were closing in on Nicholas Dirk, circling like sharks. It wasn't safe to be around when there was blood in the water.

She could almost taste the sharp edge of danger as she sipped microbrewed beer.

"I don't believe we've met. I'm Nicholas Dirk."

"Abby Nelson."

At first glance, Dirk wasn't particularly striking. He was of average height and build, with dark brown hair and a tanned complexion. His eyes, however, were remarkable. The light amber of the irises glowed yellow. A tiger's eyes. Nicholas Dirk was a predator.

As Abby shook his manicured hand, her instincts warned her that Nicholas was dangerous—fully capable of arranging the attack on Mac and Jess at the rapids. This was the sort of man who might order a murder the way others request a side of bacon with breakfast.

His jaw clenched in a smile as he greeted Mac and inquired after Jess's recovery.

Abby saw the tension in Mac's face and heard his struggle to maintain cover as he cleared his throat several times.

"I've heard," Dirk said in a low, smooth voice, "that you're a police officer. Is that right, Mac?"

"Homicide detective."

"Interesting work. Do you find it satisfying?"

"Very much so." Mac keyed his voice to the same low, slightly threatening level. "It pleases me to see criminals brought to justice."

Abby watched these two men taking each other's measure, squaring off. If Dirk was as high up in the illegal drug trade as Leo seemed to think, he was hugely powerful. Though Mac was the better man, the odds were against him.

Hoping to defuse the conflict building between them, she eased closer to Dirk. "Your house is magnificent. Was that a Chagall I saw in the foyer?"

"A copy." His words were tinged with a bit of an accent. Russian? "The original—

which I also own—is on display at the Denver Art Museum."

"You're a philanthropist. How wonderful!" Stroking his ego, she gave him an inviting smile. This sophisticated level of flirting suited her more than the blatant slut approach she used as Vanessa. "And Jess mentioned that you contribute to the Vail ski patrol."

"I try to do my civic duty."

"What other organizations do you support?"

"A homeless shelter in Denver. Rehab centers…"

Both were places where drug addicts might end up. Was Nicholas Dirk massaging his guilt with charity?

"…the Police Athletic League." Dirk's yellow gaze slid toward Mac. "The fund for widows and children of officers killed in the line of duty."

Abby could see Mac begin to bristle. She changed the subject. "Tell me more about this fantastic house. Was it built to your own specifications?"

"The original property, in the alpine chalet style, was constructed in the sixties," he said. "I've made modifications and added several rooms. Would you like the grand tour?"

"I'd be delighted."

His offer was exactly what she had hoped for. Not only would she and Mac get an idea of the layout in this house, but she might get a few more minutes to tease information from Dirk.

The grand tour took a while to organize because several other partygoers wanted to come along. Abby stepped back and observed. Though she tried to spot the bugs and surveillance cameras, only one near the foyer was readily apparent. There had to be more. But they were cleverly concealed. Of course, they would be. No expense had been spared in decorating this house. The security system had to be equally high-tech.

Her attention turned to the crowd. Some were obviously wealthy. There was an aging film actor and a rock star. And several locals. Mac was kept busy with people who had known him when he was younger. She noticed that Vince Elliot seemed to be deep in conversation with an attractive Asian woman. Leo had gone outside to stand on the spacious cedar deck with the other smokers. He tilted his head back in a chortle that Abby knew was fake…like all his other emotions. What had she ever seen in him? His swagger disgusted her. And she was glad she wasn't close enough to overhear what he was saying, probably using the Bostonian accent that he thought sounded uppercrust.

"He's not bad-looking," Mac said as he joined her.

"Who?"

He leaned close and whispered, "Your former fiancé. The guy I shot."

"Wish I knew why he was here."

"Do you want me to ask him?" A muscle in his jaw twitched. "I'm real good with ex-lovers."

She could tell that he was spoiling for a fight. Not a good plan. Lightly, she stroked his cheek. "I'd rather keep you close to me."

"Actually, I came to get you. The grand tour is about to begin."

They joined the group, escorted by Dirk, and climbed a dramatic oak staircase to the second floor where there were several beautifully furnished bedrooms and bathrooms. They climbed another staircase. This sprawling house was built into the mountainside like stairsteps. Each level went up the hill but they were all first floors with a view through the trees trunks in the surrounding forest. This level seemed entirely devoted to recreation. There was a screening room for movies, an exercise room, sauna and hot tubs. Off to one side was a full gynmasium with a basketball court. Unbelievable! The cost for heating this place must be astronomical.

On the next level was a library and meditation room with a wall of windows and a waterfall.

Though impressed by the sheer excess of a home where every whim could be indulged, Abby didn't see what she was looking for until she glanced down a short corridor toward a closed door. Outside the door was a keypad with a red light, indicating the door was locked.

One of the women on the tour—an inebriated redhead—pointed down a hallway on this highest level. "What's back there?"

"My office," Dirk said. "I'm afraid that's off-limits. That door stays locked."

"Sounds boring, anyway." She fluffed her

bottle-red hair, stumbled a bit and whined, "I need another drink, Dirk."

"Perhaps you've had enough alcohol."

"I wouldn't mind something different. Maybe a little something that I could smoke or snort."

Dirk's yellow eyes flared with momentary anger. He made a subtle gesture, and a muscular young man responded, escorting the redhead from the room. Dirk said, "Drugs are for fools."

Abby found this duality fascinating. By all reports, Dirk was a drug lord. Yet, he supported charities that dealt with addicts. And he disdained drug use in his home.

She stepped up beside him. "You sound like someone who's had experience with narcotics."

"It's a long, ugly story," he said. "One you don't want to hear."

"We've got all night." And she needed to know more about him. Lightly, she touched his arm and tugged. The muscles beneath his cashmere sweater were rock-hard. "Please sit with me. I'd like to hear more about you."

As the rest of the group spread out across

the floors, he joined her on a sofa. "Are you always so curious?"

"Always." Her smile was calculated to be encouraging. She leaned toward him. "Please tell me your story. Start at the very beginning."

"My mother was from Ukraine. She was timid. Not a very social person."

"Did you live in Denver?" Abby asked.

He nodded. "There is a large Russian and Ukrainian community in Denver, but my mother had few friends. She was lonely." His yellow eyes glowed. "This is the part of my story that could become tedious. I could speak of my father's infidelity. My mother's pathetic addiction. First from prescriptions. Then on the street. I could tell you of many years when she declined. She lost her radiant beauty."

"It must have been hard for you," Abby said.

"My mother was weak." He shrugged. "I should have paid more attention to her. Also to my sister who shared my mother's failings. Both are dead."

If anyone else had confided such a tragic story, Abby's heart would have gone out to them. But Dirk seemed detached from his family's sad history—even a bit irritated. His body language and facial expressions were incredibly hard to read. She had never encountered anyone who was so emotionally shut down. "I find it interesting that you now support rehab facilities and homeless shelters."

"I also hire many reformed addicts for my construction projects." He gestured dismissively. "Perhaps from guilt."

"Perhaps you're able to make a difference in the lives of these people."

"Or not." Abruptly, he rose from the sofa. "I'm being a bad host. We should return to the party."

As he quickly strode away from her, Abby shuddered. Nicholas Dirk was a scary person. She wanted to finish this investigation as quickly as possible.

When she rejoined Mac, she said, "The office. We should try to get inside Dirk's office."

"But it's locked."

As if that had ever stopped her before. In her purse, Abby carried a number of innocent-looking implements that could be used to gain access to Dirk's private study. The keypad locking system would be difficult to override, but it wouldn't be her first time at breaking and entering.

Chapter Twelve

Nearing midnight, the party showed no sign of ending. As some people left, Mac counted others arriving. He'd talked to the head of the Vail ski patrol, a café owner and a couple of guys he went to high school with.

Once or twice, he forgot about their investigation and enjoyed himself. Dirk was a bad guy but he threw a hell of a fine party, surrounding himself with all these salt-of-the-earth people. No matter how hard Mac tried, he couldn't see the locals as suspects, even though some of them obviously worked here. None of these people would have taken dead aim at him or at Jess. It just wasn't possible.

The jazz piano player drifted into a slow tune, and couples started dancing. Abby glided into his arms. Apparently, she'd forgotten that he wasn't a dancer. But his clumsiness didn't matter. All he had to do was hold her in a warm embrace and shuffle his feet. A pleasure.

He brushed his lips against her silky blond hair, and the clean fragrance of her shampoo tickled his senses. Tonight, she'd played her role as an heiress to perfection— cool and classy with just enough sexiness to be intriguing.

She leaned close to his ear and whispered. "We should make our move now. Dirk took another group on the grand tour. We can mingle with them."

Mac crashed back to reality. He wasn't at this party for recreation. This was an investigation, possibly the most important police work he'd done in his career.

He had some reservations about breaking into Dirk's private office. Without a search warrant, none of the evidence they found could be used in court. But this time, Mac wasn't concerned about the needs of a prosecuting attorney. All he wanted was to find proof that Dirk had bribed cops and had ordered the shooting that put Jess in the hospital. "I'm ready."

With a fetching smile, she clasped his

hand and wove a path through the other couples. They moved slowly, as though they hadn't a care in the world, as though they belonged here in the midst of excessive luxury.

On the second level, which was mostly bedrooms, Mac's heartbeat accelerated. They were getting closer. To answers? Or to increased jeopardy?

There were questions he needed to ask Abby, but he couldn't talk for fear of being overheard by surveillance bugs. He pulled her close and nuzzled her ear. "The lock," he whispered.

"Silly man," she said in a normal voice. "I've thought of that."

Her comment was the equivalent of: Trust Me. Which was something he never liked to do. Too often, other people made mistakes. A case in point was Sheila, his partner. "Are you sure you know what you're doing?"

"Absolutely." She gave him a wink. "I want to see that meditation room again. The one with the waterfall."

The room that was nearest Dirk's office. If anyone was listening, that was a good excuse. Decisively, Mac took the lead.

Though they passed other people along the way, they didn't see Dirk.

Approaching the office, Mac noticed that the door stood slightly ajar. The light on the keypad shone green. Somebody was in there.

This could be a lucky break. If they were discovered, they could claim that they were only exploring. Or they might be able to slip inside unnoticed, then hide and wait until whoever was inside left.

Moving soundlessly, he crept forward with Abby following closely. Mac pushed the door wider.

A voice called out, "Come on in, Abby."

"Leo," she said.

Inside the office, which was Spartan in comparison to the rest of the chalet, Leo Fisher stood behind a high-tech steel desk. Before him was a laptop computer. He turned the screen so they could see. It was downloading.

"We've got six minutes left," he said. "I blocked all transmissions from cameras and bugs for ten minutes, starting at midnight."

"How?" Abby asked.

"Flaw in the surveillance," he said. "The computer system defrags at midnight. I coded that to block. Ten minutes. Then it comes back on. If we're spotted in this room, Dirk's guards will be all over us."

"What are you after, Leo?"

"I might ask you the same thing, sweetheart." He shot Mac a glance. "I don't think we've formally met."

"Mac Granger. I'm the guy who shot you in the leg."

"Sloppy police work." A sneer curled his lip. "Or was it something else? Was I your target?"

Mac stiffened. This was the first time anyone had directly accused him of being dirty. "If I meant to kill you, we wouldn't be having this conversation."

"Why were you at the warehouse, Mac?"

"Bad timing."

In the direct light of the office, Leo looked like a man who should be in a hospital. His bloodshot eyes stared with a feverish glow. A cold sweat coated his forehead.

"You're working alone," Abby accused. "You're not assigned to this operation, are you?"

"Again, sweetie, that's the pot calling the kettle black." A harsh laugh rattled in the back of his throat. "We're both rogue agents."

"What have you learned?"

"I'm not telling you, Abby. This is my bust. I don't owe you."

"But you might need me," she said. "If you want to keep your job."

Reluctantly, he conceded, "I might."

"Even if you have evidence," she said, "you're going to need friends like me. Friends on the inside. We need to talk."

"It always has to be your way. Right, Abby?" He sneered at Mac. "She's got you wrapped around her little finger. I'm warning you, man to man, this woman is bad news."

When Mac took a step forward, she placed a restraining hand on his arm. "We don't have time for your whining, Leo. Are you going to work with us or not?"

The laptop computer made a final click, and Leo unplugged a rectangular disk that he slipped into his jacket pocket. "Meet me later. Two in the morning. In Vail village near the chairlift."

She gave a quick nod. "Let's get out of here."

Then all three piled through the office door and closed it. From the end of the corridor, Abby saw the light on the keypad lock switch from green to red. The security system was back up.

Their proximity to Dirk's office might be a clue to guards who were watching through the hidden surveillance cameras. If they expected to get out of here alive, they needed to return to their cover story. They needed a reason to be here. An alibi.

Casting a seductive gaze in Mac's direction, she clasped his hand and tugged him toward the meditation room. "Come on, darling. I'm dying to go in here."

He immediately understood what she was doing. "I can't wait to get you alone."

Inside the softly lighted meditation room, the indoor waterfall shimmered. The rushing sheet of water made soothing splashes. It would have been deeply calming if Abby's heart hadn't been hammering inside her rib cage. Her adrenaline level was high.

Mac embraced her. He kissed her.

If there were cameras observing, their passion needed to be convincing. Yet, kisses weren't the first thing on her mind.

On a dark emotional level where old resentments rooted and grew, she reacted to

Leo's interference. She hated him for the way their engagement had ended. And she feared his rogue attitude—his blind willingness to do anything to make the bust and build his reputation.

Still, she had to respect her former fiancé's talent. His plan to circumvent the computerized security system was nothing short of brilliant. The information he'd downloaded would surely provide evidence to use against Dirk. Evidence that would link to the dishonest cops. Proof of who shot Jess.

She shuddered to think of what might have happened if she and Mac had tried to break into the office using her less expert skills. Inadvertently, Leo had done them a great favor.

Mac lowered her to one of the burgundy meditation mats and stretched out beside her. His hands caressed her body. To all appearances, they were lovers. But his tension was palpable. Like her, Mac wasn't thinking about desire. He was in full battle mode, ready to take on anyone who might threaten them.

Abby couldn't let that happen. They needed to get away from here. To escape this opulent web.

Mac whispered, "It's time to call in the authorities."

"Not yet."

"We need a search warrant."

"On what basis?" Thus far, they'd neither seen nor heard anything that would justify a search of Dirk's chalet. If anything, he'd shown himself to be a pillar of the community.

"We'll figure it out." He tasted her lips. "I'll call my friend, Paul."

Abby didn't think the local sheriff's department was a match for Nicholas Dirk. His operation was highly sophisticated, protected by layers and layers of complexity. This investigation wasn't comparable to breaking into a small-time drug dealer's house and discovering his stash. Like it or not, they had to wait and find out what Leo had discovered.

In spite of her preoccupation, Abby felt her body responding to Mac's repeated caressing. Her consciousness began to fade into sensual incoherence.

She exhaled a soft moan as he massaged her breast. This wasn't what she wanted… but, of course, it was. She longed for his touch. "Slow down, Mac."

"But we're lovers."

The cover story. "Please, I—"

"Abby, I can't keep my hands off you."

This was part of their investigation. The best part.

In spite of her reservations and her logic, a seductive warmth rippled through her, echoing the melodic lapping of the waterfall. Now was not the time for mindless ecstasy, but when his erection rubbed against her thigh, the warmth became a flame. She dragged him on top of her, welcoming the weight of his body.

Just as suddenly, he pulled away.

They were not alone in the meditation room.

Nicholas Dirk stood in the doorway. His yellow eyes glowed like pure evil. "Get up."

Abby struggled to pull herself together. Had his cameras seen them in the office? Had Leo's foolproof plan failed? She couldn't think, couldn't come up with a glib excuse. She was tongue-tied.

Mac helped her to her feet. Gently, he brushed her hair away from her forehead. His gaze was steady and reassuring. With his arm wrapped protectively around her waist, he turned to face Dirk. "I apologize for disrespecting your hospitality. We shouldn't have come to this meditation room."

"I expect more restraint from a police officer." Dirk entered the room. His step was soundless as he prowled between the mats on the floor. "I've noticed, through the night, how you've limited your intake of alcohol."

"I need to be sober," Mac said. "I knew I'd be driving."

"You came to my home to meet me." Dirk continued to circle. At the waterfall, he stretched out his hand and allowed the liquid stream to drizzle through his opened fingers. "You asked Jess to make a special effort to arrange this meeting. And I opened my doors to you. Welcomed you."

Instead of throwing out excuses and mending their cover story, Abby stared blankly at the sparkling droplets of water. A shudder ripped through her. She was afraid to speak, afraid her voice would quaver. *Afraid!*

"Are you all right?" Mac asked.

Dumbly, she nodded.

Mac could see that she was far from okay. The color had drained from her cheeks, and she was trembling so hard that her teeth chattered. Mac was on his own with Nicholas Dirk.

Clearing his throat, he reminded himself to stick to their cover story. He looked directly into Dirk's yellow eyes. "Thank you for inviting us. You've been a very good host."

"I enjoy sharing my hospitality."

"You're a real generous guy."

Mac knew he should toss out another phony compliment, and ask about possible investment opportunities. Stick to your cover story. Soon enough, after they met with Leo later tonight, they'd have evidence to use against Dirk.

But Mac was tired of the lies. He had a bone to pick with Nicholas Dirk. Several bones, in fact. A whole damn carcass.

"Generous," Mac repeated. "That's what Lisa Hammond says."

"You know Lisa." It was a statement not a question.

"I used to know her well. She was my first real girlfriend," Mac said. "And I have to wonder… Does her daughter—*your daughter*—think you're generous? Do you ever see that little girl?"

Taken aback, Dirk yanked his hand away from the water. "I prefer not to interfere in the child's upbringing."

"Her name is Heather," Mac said.

"I'm aware of that."

"You take care of your daughter the way you contribute to rehab centers and the Police Athletic League. From a distance. Your hands stay clean. You think you can't be touched."

"What are you implying?"

Mac stepped away from Abby and moved closer to Nicholas Dirk. "How much do you know about the law?"

"I have attorneys." Dirk's slight accent grew more pronounced; he was getting ticked off. "They handle such affairs."

"The law is all about intent," Mac said.

"I'm aware of that."

"Your finger might *not* have pulled the trigger, but if you intended harm, you're guilty." Mac stretched out his arm and reached into the waterfall, mocking Dirk's gesture, gliding his hand through the flow. "No amount of sparkling spring water can wash that guilt away."

Dirk's eyes narrowed to amber slits. "What did you expect to gain by meeting me?"

"I'm looking for the truth."

"Given your current reputation at the Denver police department, that request is ironic."

He knew! Dirk knew that Mac was accused of taking bribes. But, of course, he'd know. Dirk was the man who paid the bribes; he had a cop on the inside to feed him information. This yellow-eyed bastard might be the only person—other than the dirty cop—who knew the truth. "You know my reputation is clean."

"How could I know? And why would I care?" Dirk strode from the room. As he left, he nodded to a young man who waited outside. "Show these people to the door."

With an effort, Mac controlled the anger that surged wildly through his veins. He wanted to lash out against Nicholas Dirk, to tear that smug, taunting expression from his face. But there was nothing Mac could do— not in this household that was swarming with Dirk's henchmen. If there hadn't been all these party-time witnesses, Dirk could have used this opportunity to finish the job his hired assassin had started at the rapids.

As Mac strode silently through the house, Abby slipped her hand into his. Her flesh was ice-cold, and he glanced down at her. Her dark brown eyes were wide. There was a tension around her mouth as if she were suppressing a cry.

He leaned down toward her. "It's okay, Abby."

"Let's just get out of here."

In the vaulted foyer, they picked up their coats. Their escort pointed them toward the wrought iron gateway, and they walked past the two guards without being stopped. "Nothing to worry about," he said to Abby. "We're home free."

After taking a few more steps, she halted. Her hand rested on her breast and she was breathing hard as she sank down on the thigh-high stone wall that surrounded the chalet. "Give me a minute."

When he tried to sit beside her, she waved him away. "I need space," she said.

Mac leaned against the trunk of a pine tree beside the wall and watched her with concern. It almost seemed like she was frightened. A perfectly sane response. They'd been in danger.

Unfortunately, he hadn't handled the cover story well. Instead of appearing harmless, he practically came right out and accused Dirk of shooting Jess. *Damn it!* Undercover work just wasn't his thing. "Abby, I didn't mean to—"

"Give me a minute to catch my breath."

A minute passed. Then another. And another.

Mac watched as another couple left the party and went to their car. Then, he spotted Leo walking beside Vince Elliot. They were headed in the opposite direction down the road. Seeing the two undercover agents together started the wheels turning in Mac's brain. Were they working together? Though they spoke quietly, the conversation seemed heated. Vince gestured repeatedly.

A third man came through the gates. He moved stealthily in the same direction as Vince and Leo, edging close to them. Then he paused in the shadow of a pine tree.

Mac watched with interest. It appeared that the third man was eavesdropping on Vince and Leo. Likely, he was one of Dirk's men, hoping to overhear the conversation between the two undercover operatives.

Before Mac could move closer, Leo got into his car. The door slammed. Vince stalked away.

The third man, still in shadow, struck a match to light his cigarette. In the flare of the match, Mac caught a glimpse of his features. He looked familiar, but Mac couldn't put a name to that face. The smoker could have been somebody local, somebody Mac knew in high school. But that identification didn't fit. Was he from Denver? Another cop?

The smoker quickly walked to his vehicle, got inside and drove away fast in the same direction as Leo.

Finally, Abby stood. "Sorry," she muttered, "I don't know what came over me."

"Short of breath. Cold. Pale." Mac enumerated her symptoms. "Needing space. Feeling—"

"All right," she snapped. "Maybe I had a little panic attack."

Stiffly, Abby stalked past him toward the car. Nothing like this had ever happened to her before. *A panic attack.* When she was working alone, she never experienced fear. *Never.* She was self-possessed. In control.

But she had been afraid, desperately afraid. Even now, she felt the residual effects.

Her throat was tight. Her body, cold. As they drove away from the well-lit mansion, a gasp escaped her lips.

"Are you okay?" Mac asked.

"Fine."

That was a lie. She'd lost her ability to function in an undercover situation. For the first time in her career, she'd been crippled by fear.

Mac drove until they had returned to a more populated area. He pulled into a convenience store parking lot and turned to her. "Tell me what's wrong."

She saw the concern on his face. The sincerity. Though she wanted to brush off her panic attack, she couldn't lie to that face. "Okay, I'll admit that I was scared. Really scared."

Mac reached toward her and stroked her cheek. "Nicholas Dirk is a scary guy."

"I've been in danger before," she said. "And I never felt like this."

"It's okay, Abby."

His voice was so gentle that she wanted to cry. *Swell!* Not only was she a scaredy cat but a crybaby as well. *Pull it together, girl.*

Mac squeezed her fingers and smiled encouragement. There was nothing condescending about his gesture. He still respected her. He cared about her.

She cared about him, too. And that was her big, fat problem. His safety was more important than their investigation. If anything happened to him, she couldn't bear it. "I don't want to lose you."

"I'm not going anywhere."

"Please, Mac. Let's stop investigating right now." She fought the tears that ached behind her eyelids. "We can take what we know and call for a search warrant. That's what you wanted, isn't it?"

"I changed my mind," Mac said. "I think we should meet Leo."

"Let him handle it," she pleaded. "Let him have his precious bust."

"He can take the credit. I don't care about that." Mac frowned. "His break-in scheme of overriding the surveillance system was brilliant, but your ex-fiancé looks pretty damned crazy to me. I don't trust him to do the right thing."

She had to agree. Leo had lost track of his boundaries and was, therefore, unpredictable. "He's been undercover too long."

"Tell me about him. Tell me what to expect when we meet. Can we trust him?"

"No."

Pulling away from Mac, she leaned back in the passenger seat and stared through the windshield at the brightly lit entrance to the convenience store. She knew what she had to say, knew how to explain Leo's erratic personality. But their breakup was an embarrassing moment she'd never shared with anyone else.

"Leo has been on the edge for a long time," she said. "We broke up eighteen months ago. Fourth of July. We'd both completed undercover assignments and were planning to spend a week together at his apartment in Brooklyn."

She remembered her excitement. They were going to behave like a normal couple, maybe go to dinner, maybe watch a fireworks display. "I baked a cake and frosted it. Red, white and blue."

"You cook?"

"Not often. But when I do, I make everything from scratch. Like a big project."

She didn't look at Mac, and he kept his distance. Apparently, he sensed that this was hard for her.

Abby continued, "When Leo came through the door, he was still in character, acting the part of a macho drug dealer. I could see it in the way he swaggered. And I teased him. I told him to leave his work at the office."

The next part was the most painful. "He snapped at me, warned me to back off. But I didn't." On her lap, her fingers twisted in a knot. "He slapped me. Hard. I fell to the floor. He kicked me. And then he took my cake, my beautiful cake, and dumped it in the sink."

"Bastard," Mac muttered.

She concluded, "I walked out the door and never looked back."

When his hand touched her shoulder, she couldn't hold back. She dove toward him and buried her face against his expensive new jacket.

Leo's abuse nearly destroyed her self-confidence. Abby had never thought of herself as the kind of woman who got herself into a situation where she'd be slapped around. All she'd wanted was a normal relationship, but that simple happiness had eluded her...until she met Mac.

He wasn't like anyone she'd ever known. He was solid, honest and strong.

A tear slipped down her cheek. With Mac, she didn't have to pretend to be someone else. All the emotions she covered up while doing her professional duty could be expressed. Her sadness. Her joy. And her fear.

"I want this to be over."

"Soon," he promised. "Very soon."

Chapter Thirteen

As the 2:00 a.m. meeting drew near, Mac took every precaution. He drove for miles on a circuitous route to make sure no one was following. Instead of parking at the underground lot outside Vail village, he took a service road onto the slopes. The last couple of miles, he turned off the headlights and wove slowly through the forested area. Finally, he parked.

"Where are we?" Abby asked.

Her voice sounded stronger—even a bit irritated. And he was glad. He'd rather have her grumpy than scared to death. "We're at the edge of the ski runs that lead into town. Nobody will find us here." He gave her an assessing look. "How are you doing?"

"I'm better," she said.

"If you want to stay in the car and wait while I meet Leo, that's fine."

"Not a chance."

Before he could say another word, she was out of the car. She paused at the edge of the trees. With her shining blond hair covered by a cap and her jacket zipped all the way to her throat, she seemed ready for action.

Soft moonlight shone on her face, and Mac tried to read her expression. Her delicate features were set in stone, revealing nothing. He couldn't tell if she'd conquered her panic. Abby continued to baffle him with her many identities. "Tell me what you're thinking."

"I need to be with you when you meet Leo," she said. "In case you have to negotiate with him."

"I can handle it."

"This shouldn't be dangerous. It's only Leo."

"He worries me more than anybody else." Especially after hearing how he'd abused Abby. In Mac's book, Leo Fisher was lower than the dirt beneath his boots.

"He's going to be a pain in the butt," she said. "It won't be easy to convince him to give us a copy of that disk he downloaded."

"Even if he does agree, how will it be

possible to make a copy? It's the middle of the night."

"I figure Leo wanted to meet in Vail village because he's staying nearby. We'll go back to his room—where I'm sure he has a computer. And he can make a copy."

Her plan sounded simple and rational. Leo would get credit for his bust. And they'd use the disk to find the names of the dirty cops. "Leo won't like sharing."

Her eyes narrowed. "He owes me."

"So do I." His words were heartfelt. "I never would have gotten this far without your help."

"It's the least I can do." A thin smile touched her lips. "I should have known from the first minute I saw you that the accusations were wrong. I should have filed an immediate report that said, 'Met Mac. He's clean.'"

"No one would have believed you," he said. Even Lieutenant Perkins had thought he was dirty. "I'm glad you didn't handle your assignment that way."

"Why?"

"If you filed too fast, I never would have gotten the chance to know you. To care for you. To make love to you!"

She stepped into his waiting arms, and her slender body molded perfectly against him. Though they were different, they fit together well.

The chill night air whispered through the pines, lightly caressing them. And he wished he could forget the investigating and devote himself entirely to Abby. Breaking down the barriers she constructed around herself. Watching her smile. Making love to her again and again.

"We should go," she said. "It's almost two."

They followed the dirt path leading out of the trees. In less than a month, this slope would be snow-covered, populated by downhill skiers. As they stepped onto the open ski run, he looked down at the lights of the village. It was charming. A picture postcard.

A clattering noise attracted his attention, and he looked up and to the right. The chair-lift cables clattered against the steel support poles. "This would be a faster descent if we were skiing. Do you ski?"

"Once or twice," she said. "I like the sensation of speed. The wind in my face. But I'm not very good."

"Opening day is a lot of fun," he said. "I'd like to take you skiing."

She paused. "Are you asking me for a date?"

"I want to see you again, Abby."

Her grin was tinged with sadness. "Me, too."

He didn't want to think about what would happen after she moved on to her next assignment. Her departure was inevitable, but the idea that she would leave him caused an ache in his gut. He didn't want her to go.

Near the bottom of the slope, they passed several pieces of heavy equipment parked in a cleared area. "It's a bad time for new construction," Mac said. "They're not going to get much done before the winter snow."

She squinted through the dark at a dump truck. "Take a look at that logo. These trucks belong to Dirk Development."

Apparently, Dirk had some legitimate business as well as his nefarious activity. "Criminal diversification?"

"A land development business is a good way to launder his drug money," she said.

They hiked through the moonlight into the village. Though there were a few Friday night revelers, the streets were mostly deserted as they neared the coffee shop near the chairlift where they were supposed to meet Leo.

Mac heard a muffled thud and a groan. Protectively, he eased Abby back against the wall of a juice shop that had closed hours ago. He took his gun from the ankle holster.

Staying close to the wall, he edged his way to the corner and peered toward the coffee shop. Leo slumped against a streetlamp. His gun was in his hand. Weakly, he aimed in the opposite direction and fired twice.

"Leo," Abby called to him.

He groaned. "Stay back."

Mac took charge. Again, he was in a shoot-out situation. This time, he would make no mistake. "Abby, stay here. Lay down a line of fire to distract from Leo. I'm going over there to get another angle."

She followed his instructions, expertly stepping away from the wall and firing in the direction Leo had aimed. Then, she stepped back.

Mac darted across the street. From this vantage point, he caught sight of a figure dressed in black, wearing a knit cap low on the forehead.

For one stunned moment, Mac hesitated. A little more than a week ago, he'd killed Dante Williams at the warehouse. He didn't want another death on his conscience.

The black-clad figure raised an arm and pointed a handgun with a silencer at Leo. Mac had no choice. He aimed low and fired. Though well within range, he missed.

Impossible! Mac was an expert marksman who seldom missed. He looked down at the gun. This wasn't his weapon; it was Abby's. Though it didn't seem possible with all her high tech equipment, the gun was defective. The trigger was tight. The sight was off. Damn it! He might as well be unarmed.

The figure retreated.

Leo had forced himself to a standing posture. Again, he fired his weapon wildly. Then he staggered toward Abby. He took another hit. His body jerked.

Mac calculated the direction of the shot. Peering through the light and shadow on the streets, he spied the silhouette of the shooter reflected against a shop window.

Mac fired. Twice. And he watched the figure move away unharmed.

Abby's gun was worthless. All it could do was make noise. Mac should have taken target practice, should have been better prepared.

Leo fell. He was close to Abby, and she pulled him around the corner to safety.

Mac dashed across the street. He crouched over Abby, protecting her and Leo. He didn't bother calling 911. Even at this late hour, the village was well patrolled. "The sheriff ought to be here in a minute," he said. "Hang on, Leo."

"The disk." Leo reached inside his jacket. His chest was drenched in blood. His breath rattled in his throat. Struggling, he handed a mangled envelope to Abby. "I get credit for this bust."

"Absolutely," she said.

"Remember that." Leo held up his hand, smeared with gore. He was dying. "I'm the best."

His eyelids winced shut. He stiffened, then his body went slack.

"Leo," Abby whispered. She looked up at Mac with a horror-stricken expression. "What should we do?"

Mac felt for a pulse. Nothing. Leo Fisher

was gone. The abusive bastard had died in Abby's arms.

"Give me the disk," Mac said.

She handed him the torn, bloody envelope. Even before Mac tore it open, he knew what he would find. The small plastic disk had been shattered by the assassin's bullet. It was worthless.

Though they were in an idyllic mountain village, this moment was a replay of the shoot-out at the seedy Denver warehouse. Sudden violence. Gunfire. A man was dead. And the evidence had been destroyed.

Mac remembered the aftermath of the warehouse shooting. He was the suspect. His reputation was ruined. And now, he stood over the body of a man he'd already shot before.

Nobody would believe his presence here was mere coincidence. If Mac had been the investigating officer on this case, he would have suspected…himself. This was more than bad timing. He'd been framed. It was all happening again. A grim déjà vu. He needed to get the hell away from here.

As soon as the thought crossed his mind, he heard a muffled gunshot. The window of the shop behind them shattered. Whoever killed Leo was after them.

Abby stood and took aim. She fired until her clip was empty. With his weapon defective, and hers empty, they were virtually unarmed.

Abby was on her feet. Together, they darted around the corner onto a winding street where lighted storefronts made concealment difficult. It was best to keep moving through this maze of boutiques and cafés until they found their way to the open slopes.

"What about Leo?" Abby asked.

He was gone. Mac knew it, and so did she. "There's nothing we can do for him."

Together, they ran toward the covered bridge crossing Gore Creek. A good hiding place. Too good.

"Wait," he said. Abby skidded to a halt beside him.

Just as he had followed her instructions when it came to undercover work, she did as he ordered, ceding authority to him. No petty argument. No question.

As they watched the bridge, a figure in black stepped away from the shadows, opened fire and slipped back inside the covered bridge.

Mac's weapon was useless. They had to run.

Racing past the clock tower, they circled all the way back to the chairlift. Flattened against a shadowed wall, they watched and waited.

Police sirens echoed through the valley. There were shouts on the street. Local law enforcement had arrived on the scene.

Mac's training told him to go back, to turn himself in and be taken into custody. That was the right thing to do, and he was a man who always played by the rules. A homicide detective. A good cop.

But he didn't know who to trust or where to turn. The local sheriff could be dirty. All Mac had for evidence was a broken computer disk. Why should they believe him when Nicholas Dirk was a respected member of the community?

Like it or not, Mac was on his own. "Stay here, Abby. I'm going to run."

"I'm coming with you."

"You'll be safer if—"

"No way. I already made my decision. It's you and me, Mac."

A surge of adrenaline momentarily boosted

his confidence. To escape, they needed a distraction. "I've got an idea. Stay close."

They ran across the open space to the operator's booth for the chairlift. Using the butt of Abby's defective gun, he broke the window in the door, reached inside and twisted the lock. He'd worked in this booth through high school, and knew how the equipment operated. After he flipped a couple of switches, the machinery rumbled, and the chairlift went into motion. It was one hell of a distraction.

Instead of taking one of the chairs to the upper slopes, he led Abby through the door beside the swooping metal chairs. They leaped down from the platform to the earth below and crouched.

Before them, the hillside beckoned. His car was parked a few hundred yards away, but the approach to it was steeply uphill and there was very little cover.

Mac spoke over the noise of the lift. "We'll go to the construction area where Dirk's trucks are parked. I'll cover you."

Abby took off running, and he followed. He kept looking over his shoulder, watching the shadows, knowing an assassin waited. He spied a dark figure outlined in the glow of a streetlamp.

Without bothering to aim, Mac spent another couple of bullets, and the gunman dodged.

If he came after them, he stood a good chance of picking them off before they reached Mac's car.

At the construction site, Mac pulled Abby behind the dump truck with the Dirk Development logo on the door. They were both gasping for breath.

"We need to make a stand," he said.

"If that means no more running uphill, I'm for it."

He reached up and tried the door handle on the truck. Locked. He scanned the site. His gaze lit on the bulldozer. One summer, he'd worked construction and had the chance to drive one of these big machines that moved on a crawler tractor like an army tank.

"Over here, Abby."

She trotted behind him and watched as he climbed up onto the track roller. He reached down to help her up.

"You're joking." Still, she took his hand

and allowed him to pull her up. "This isn't exactly a subtle getaway vehicle."

He pulled her onto the tractor. "I've run one of these before. Summer job."

"Why couldn't you just work at a burger joint like a normal teenager?"

He sat in the driver's seat of the cab. As he had hoped, the key was in the ignition. There were two levers in front of him and more switches and levers beside the armrests. Some of them moved the blade in the front. Others turned the dozer left and right. He didn't exactly remember which did what.

Abby leaned over his shoulder. "How are we going to do this?"

"We wait. When we see the shooter, we make a run at him."

"You want to attack him with a bull-dozer?"

"It'll work."

"No way," she said. "I say we run toward the car on our own two feet."

"With our backs exposed for a hundred yards? We'll never make it."

She hovered silently behind him, and they waited.

In the village, the chairlift had been turned

off. Though there was a commotion on the streets of Vail, the hillsides were quiet.

He heard a footstep crunch on the dried grasses. Peering through the moonlight, he saw a dark figure creeping stealthily, glancing left and right, searching. In that instant, Mac recognized their assailant; he was the same man—the smoker—who had followed Leo and Vince when they left the party.

And he was close.

Now! Mac switched the bulldozer on. He turned on the headlights, bathing their assailant in light. As the gunman threw up his arms to protect himself from the glare, Mac yanked on the throttle. The blade of the dozer slapped up and down. They lurched forward, churning clumsily over uneven earth.

The assailant dodged. But they were almost on top of him. Mac heard a shout. Maybe he'd finally hurt this guy.

The dozer was headed uphill toward the car. But they were moving too fast. Mac slammed his foot on the brake pedal, but they didn't stop. He wrenched the levers, barely missing a boulder.

"Turn it off," Abby shouted.

"I forgot how."

He couldn't make the tanklike machinery do what he wanted. It rampaged across the land, charging up the hill. Frantically, Mac flipped switches and levers.

The engine squealed. It was in the wrong gear. Going too fast. The lowered blade scooped up a ton of rocks.

Mac slammed every lever until the dozer stopped. Smoke poured from the front grille.

He turned off the headlights.

They ran the last twenty yards to the car.

Abby slammed the passenger door as she got in beside him. "That was the most half-witted escape plan I've ever seen."

"But we're here."

They were on the run. He drove along the service road leading away from Vail, aware that he was fleeing the scene of the crime. How the hell had he gotten himself into this position?

Mac was one of the good guys. He'd always been on the right side of the law. In scores of homicide investigations, he'd disdained excuses from wrong-doers. The choice between right and wrong was clear.

Only the guilty go on the run.

Chapter Fourteen

The assassin limped back toward the condo where he was staying near Vail village. All that gunfire, and he hadn't been hit. But he'd badly sprained his ankle when Mac Granger charged at him with a bulldozer. A freaking bulldozer!

This night had been one freaking disaster after another. After he'd followed Leo Fisher and Vince Elliot from the party and overheard that Leo had a disk of all the information on Dirk's computer, the necessary action was clear. *Get the disk.*

But Leo had proved to be a difficult adversary, immediately aware of being tailed. It had taken all kinds of maneuvers to get close to him. On the streets of the village, Leo was armed and wary. He had to be shot.

Then Mac and Abby showed before the assassin could retrieve the disk.

Damn them! He wanted them dead. Both of them.

Leaning heavily on the wooden railing, he climbed the stairs to the second-floor condo. The door swung wide. His two coconspirators were waiting.

"What the hell happened?" asked a rumbling voice. "From all those sirens, it sounds like every cop in the county is in the village."

The assassin staggered past the kitchenette and collapsed in a chair. He reached for his cigarettes. "Leo's dead. Mac and Abby have the disk."

"We're in deep trouble. Our names are going to pop up on Dirk's list of contacts." The most senior of the three, a heavyset man, paced nervously. "The local cops are probably running that computer information right now."

"Not yet." The assassin took a long drag on his cigarette. His ankle was killing him. It might have been easier to be shot. "They're on the run. Mac and Abby."

It didn't make sense. With the computer disk, Mac had the proof he needed. He had the evidence that would ultimately be their undoing.

"Why would Mac run?"

"Maybe he finally got smart." The injured man took a drag on his cigarette. "Mac could sell that disk back to Dirk for a substantial amount."

"Not Mac," said the youngest of the three. "He's totally straight. Not a blackmailer."

"Maybe he's changed," the smoker said. "At Dirk's party, he was wearing new clothes. Expensive stuff. And he was talking about moving back to the mountains."

"I don't believe it."

"You haven't seen the way he acts around that woman, Abby. He's got the hots for her. And a man in love does crazy things."

"Suppose you're right and Mac tries to blackmail Dirk. Where does that leave us?"

The heavyset man growled, "We can't wait around and hope everything works out."

"Agreed." The smoker stared down at his sprained ankle. Taking off his boot would be incredibly painful. "We have to get Mac before he gets us. The problem is, how do we find him?"

"He might go to stay with his friend."

"The deputy?" The smoker twisted around in the chair to get comfortable. He unclipped the holster from his belt. It was empty. He'd disposed of the gun he used on Leo very deliberately. "Mac can't stay with a cop. The cops are going to be looking for him."

"He could move in with another friend. He seems to know everybody around here."

"Yeah, he's Mister Popular. The prodigal son returned."

"What about that old girlfriend of his?"

"Negative," the smoker said. "Not while he's got Abby with him."

"He's got other family in the area," said the younger conspirator. "I happen to know that his mother's maiden name was Mac-Cloud."

The heavyset man spread a map of the area on the counter in the kitchenette. "We should be able to figure this out. We're cops. We know how to do a search."

"And what do we do when we find him?"

"The same thing we've been trying to do from the start." An angry frown creased the big man's broad forehead. "We kill the son of a bitch. It'd be nice if we could make it look like an accident, like Mac had been killed by his own stupidity."

"What about the woman?"

"We kill her, too."

A bloody solution. But there was no other way. None of them wanted to spend the rest of their days in prison.

MILE AFTER MILE, Abby stared through the windshield. The Colorado night closed more tightly around them as Mac turned onto a narrow road through an old-growth forest. The trees were so thick that it felt like they'd entered a tunnel. She had no idea where they were or where they were going. As long as they were safe, she didn't care.

But that safety was too tenuous. Leo had died a violent death in her arms—a victim of his own rogue ambition. He had wanted to be the best and died proving his claim. And what had his efforts earned him? He'd probably receive a special commendation—his name on the plaque of FBI service martyrs, killed in the line of duty. It wasn't enough—not worth his life.

Abby knew how close she and Mac had come to joining Leo. It was a miracle they'd escaped without injury. "We should have turned ourselves in."

"We were under assault by a sniper," Mac

reminded her. "We had to keep moving. We had to run."

"But now?" She turned toward him. The lights from the dashboard reflected off his stubborn jaw. "We should go back. You could talk to your friend, Paul Hemmings. We'd be treated fairly."

"Yeah, sure," he said bitterly. "Like I was treated fairly after the shooting at the Denver warehouse. I'm not going back until I have dead-on proof of my own innocence."

"We could help the police investigate."

"How? We have no evidence against Dirk, no legal cause for a search warrant. There's no way to link the assassin in the village with Nicholas Dirk."

"There has to be something."

"In this case, law enforcement is powerless." His fingers tightened on the steering wheel. "There's nothing more goddamned frustrating than watching a murderer go free. I've seen it too many times before. They get off on a technicality. Or they have a clever attorney. And they walk."

"It happens."

"Not this time." A grim smile touched

the edge of his mouth. "Not while we have this disk."

"But it's shattered."

"Dirk doesn't know the disk was destroyed."

Apprehension twisted in her gut. Abby knew she wasn't going to like what came next. "Please don't tell me you're thinking about a sting."

"That's exactly what I'm thinking," Mac said. "Dirk must have known about the disk. That's why he went after Leo. We can use the disk to lure him out."

She hated the recklessness of his plan. "If we go ahead with this idea—and that's a very big if—why not arrange the sting through the local police?"

"Because everybody around here loves Nicholas Dirk. His development company provides employment. He supports the local ski patrol. Nobody is going to believe who he really is."

"Okay, forget the locals. We can call in the feds. Believe me, the FBI knows how to do a sting."

For a moment, he was quiet. His attention concentrated on the twisting gravel road that climbed higher through the trees. She desperately hoped that he was considering her idea. If she contacted her superiors, she and Mac could step back and allow the experts to take over. They might actually get out of this alive.

Mac gave a quick shake of his head. "I don't want to turn this over to the feds. They'll make a deal with Dirk, and he'll get off with protective custody. He deserves more than a slap on the wrist. I want to see him prosecuted and put in prison. He's responsible for shooting my friend, for sending the assassin who killed Leo and tried to kill us."

"You don't even know if he's guilty."

"Who else could it be? Dirk is the drug kingpin, the man with the power. He's calling the shots."

"I'm not arguing with you, Mac."

"Nicholas Dirk. And the dirty cops. They've got to pay for what they've done." He glanced toward her. "This isn't your fight, Abby. If you want out, tell me. I can take you back to town."

Obviously, that was the smart thing to do. Going along with Mac's plan meant she could kiss her career goodbye. More than that, she was risking her life on a sting operation with no backup, no escape. If Dirk and his men came in with guns blazing, what could she and Mac do? Hope for another convenient bulldozer?

But she couldn't leave him, couldn't walk away. He needed her.

As they emerged from the thick forest, he slowed the car and glided to a stop behind a small log cabin. "This is where we'll stay tonight. This place belongs to my great-aunt Lucille MacCloud."

"The woman who skis and likes fancy jewelry?"

"That's the one. She's back east visiting her daughter."

Abby stepped out of the car. "Isn't this the first place Paul would look?"

"Eventually, he'll figure it out. But we can bunk down here until morning."

Which was only a few hours away. Still, she was glad for the respite. Any sleep at all was better than none.

She followed him to the rear of the cabin which perched at the edge of steep cliff. Instead of going to the door, Mac stood at the edge of the precipice. He made a handsome figure, strong and tall, outlined by the shimmer of moonlight.

She joined him. After driving through the dense forest, stepping onto this ledge was like opening a curtain on a spectacular natural drama. The vast night sky was dotted with a million stars. The rugged hillsides spread below them. In the distance, the fading moonlight softened the jagged edges of hogbacks and tinted the landscape with a subtle blue haze.

This land was serene and magnificent—a place to put down roots and to grow. There would be no need for deception in this land, no more lies. "I could live here."

"You'd get bored."

"Did you? When you were growing up, were you bored?"

"A little." He slipped his arm around her waist. "I like the city. The stimulation. The lights. The noise."

"The life of a city cop."

"It's been a good life. But now that I'm here, the mountains are starting to grow on me." He shrugged. "I feel at peace. That sounds crazy, given what's happening. But I do."

Oddly enough, so did she. Abby knew this weird sense of well-being in the midst of danger and chaos wasn't due to the scenery. It was the bond she'd formed with Mac. Being with him had a soothing effect, as though she had finally found the place she belonged, the place she was supposed to stay. In his arms. Forever.

He pulled her close against his lean, hard body. "There are so many places I want to show you. The white-water rapids of the Roaring Fork River. A fiery red sunset on the Sangre de Christos. The morning after the first snow. There's nothing so clean and pure as that first heavy snowfall. I could teach you to ski in champagne powder."

And she longed to share these visions with him, to build on their attraction until their relationship was a reality. "It's ironic," she said. "It sounds like you've fallen in love with the mountains. Just like our cover story."

He turned her toward him. Gently, he combed his fingers through her hair. Holding her face, he tasted her lips. "Our cover story was a lie."

She wrapped her arms around his lean torso. "Sometimes, lies come true."

The night breeze whispered through her hair, and she was intensely aware of their surroundings. The rough granite surface beneath her boots. The scent of sticky resin from the pines. The cries of night predators. Most of all, she was aware of him. His bodily warmth drew her closer and kindled a fire deep inside her.

When she looked up at him, his face was surrounded by a night filled with stars. She offered her lips, and he kissed her with the sweet yet demanding passion she had come to expect. Was it only last night they'd made love for the first time? It seemed like they had always been together, as though they were meant to be one.

His tongue engaged with hers as he skillfully deepened their kiss. And she savored the slick interior of his mouth. He was so good at this. She wished he would never stop kissing her and holding her. She wished they could always be together. And, in this moment, she knew she couldn't abandon him…no matter how ill-fated his plans. She would follow this man to the ends of the earth and back again. He was her destiny.

Again, she studied his handsome face. His

hair shone silvery in the moonlight. "About that sting?"

"Yeah?"

"I'm in."

He swept her toward the log cabin. Reaching under the flower box in the window where a few scraggly weeds remained, he found the key to the back door.

Inside, the overhead light shone on a cozy kitchen with ancient appliances in avocado-green. Abby dragged her finger through a layer of dust that coated the countertop. "Either your great-aunt Lucille is a terrible housekeeper or she doesn't spend much time here."

"It's the latter," he said. "She's hardly ever here. For years, she's been talking about selling this cabin."

"Why doesn't she?"

"I think she's waiting for me to make her an offer. You know, to keep the place in the family."

He opened the refrigerator. Though there were condiments on the door, it was otherwise empty.

"Too bad," Abby said. "I'm famished."

He prowled toward a tall pantry cupboard

and opened it. Inside were rows and rows of canned goods. "If you want something to eat, I guess we could throw all this stuff in a pot and heat it up."

"Delightful as that sounds, I'm more tired than hungry. I vote for bed."

"Good choice."

He turned off the kitchen light and took her hand. Using only the glow through the cabin's windows, he directed her across a living room and into a small room with a big brass bed. Though quilts piled high on the mattress, the cold of the empty cabin had sunk into her bones. She shivered. "I'm too chilly to get undressed."

"Then I'll have to warm you up."

She placed a restraining palm on his chest. "Down, boy. It's really too cold."

"Then we'd better hope this thing still works." He knelt beside a three foot square metal box with vents across the front. "It's a propane-fueled heater. Not as romantic as a fireplace but efficient."

While Mac fiddled with the pilot light, Abby circled the small bedroom. A faint coat of dust dulled the surfaces of the dresser and a small desk. The cabin seemed abandoned, bereft of life. Outside the cabin door was some of the most beautiful scenery in the world. Yet, there was an emptiness about this place.

Abby recognized the atmosphere. It reminded her of the echoing silence in her apartment when she came home from an undercover assignment. It was loneliness.

The propane heater made a whooshing noise as the jets lit. Mac held his hand in front of the vents. "That should do it. We'll be toasty in no time."

She sat on the bed with her arms wrapped tightly around her and watched as he came toward her. Though they'd known each other a short time, his smile filled a space in her life that had been vacant. His presence completed her in ways she couldn't begin to comprehend, except to say that she trusted him. Mac would never lie to her, even when she didn't like what he was saying. He would never cheat.

He knelt before her and gently removed her boots. "Get under the covers, Abby."

Still fully dressed, she did as he said. The sheets were icy, and she clung to him, drawing warmth from his strength. Slowly and subtly, their embrace became erotic.

"Warmer?" Mac asked.

"Yes."

"Let's take off these jackets."

Under the covers, they wriggled out of their outer layers of clothing. She wasn't cold anymore but couldn't tell if the heat she felt was due to the propane heater or her own internal fire.

As he unbuttoned her blouse, her skin tingled. Each newly revealed inch of exposed flesh was highly sensitized. By the time they were naked, her desire had reached an impossible, unstoppable level. She needed his kisses and caresses.

Last night had been a wonderful introduction to their lovemaking. Tonight was a completion. She knew what to expect, knew that his hand would cup her breast in a firm and tantalizing grasp. Yet, her reaction to his touch caused her to gasp with delighted surprise.

When he thrust inside her, she held him. Her body twitched and trembled around him, reaching a climax that was higher than the snow-capped peaks, higher than the stars and the moon. This was pure happiness. Pure pleasure.

Abby did not float gently back to earth.

After they made love, she descended with a thud. Her exhaustion was overwhelming. Yet, her mind would not be still.

The fulfillment she shared with Mac was everything she'd ever hoped for, and she couldn't bear the thought of losing him.

Her mind flashed to Leo, dying on the village street. His death was so futile. So useless.

And Mac wanted to face the same danger. He wanted to single-handedly take on Nicholas Dirk.

This sting must not happen. Abby couldn't allow Mac to take the risk. She had to call in other law enforcement people. Even though it meant lying to Mac.

This deception was for his own good.

Chapter Fifteen

After only a few hours of sleep, Mac was awake. The faint hint of dawn crept through the blinds and curtains in the cabin bedroom. It wasn't even six o'clock.

He rolled to his side and gazed down at the beautiful face of the woman who lay beside him. Her thick eyelashes formed dark crescents above her high cheekbones. Her soft lips parted as if waiting for his kiss.

Though he didn't want to wake her, he lightly stroked the firm line of her jaw. It was hard to believe that they had ended up together. He hated manipulation, and that was her job as an undercover fed; she was a professional liar. But not to him. Not anymore.

They were a team. She was the only woman he could trust.

Her eyelids fluttered open. The world's

most beautiful smile curved her lips. "Is it morning?"

"Almost." He kissed her forehead. "I like waking up with you beside me."

Her naked arms wrapped around him. Their bodies joined. Her warm flesh rubbed against his morning erection. He wanted her, couldn't keep himself away from her. But not now. "We should probably get moving before Paul figures out that I came here."

"Would that be such a bad thing? Having your friend with us?"

"Yes," he said. By running away last night, he'd probably destroyed his career. Hers, too. "I don't want to ruin Paul's livelihood. He's got two little girls to support."

Her eyelids squeezed shut, and she gave a quick shake as though casting off the remnants of sleep. When her eyes opened, Abby was one hundred percent alert. "We need to figure out what we're doing, Mac."

When she was in his arms, he couldn't think of anything other than her delectable body. He gave her one last kiss, then slipped out from under the covers.

"Here's what we already know," he said. "Nicholas Dirk is the bad guy."

"Evidence?"

"Circumstantial," he said. "But damning."

She sat up in the bed and stretched. Her perfect round breasts enticed him, begging for his touch. Mac had to turn away as he ran through the evidence they had on Dirk. "I'll start with the attack at the rapids when Jess was shot. That happened right after we drove past Dirk's house. He sent one of his henchmen to pose as a hunter."

"Okay," she said. "That makes sense."

"Then there's Leo. All his undercover work must have pointed to Dirk. That was why he made the disk from Dirk's computer. Then Leo was killed."

"Sounds like a pretty clear connection to Dirk," she said. "But we still don't know about the dirty cops."

Moving with graceful precision, she climbed out of the bed, naked. Mac could feel his brain turning to mush, and he struggled to be coherent. "I saw Vince Elliot talking to Leo after the party."

"Which could mean they were two undercover operatives consulting with each other." She'd begun to dress herself. "They already knew each other."

"Or Vince could be dirty. But I don't think so." Mac remembered the other man who had been watching from the dark. The smoker. "There was somebody else watching them from the shadows, and I'm pretty sure that someone turned out to be the assassin who attacked us in Vail village."

Her eyebrows raised. "Why didn't you mention this before?"

"There's hasn't exactly been time for a daily briefing."

"Was this guy someone who works for Dirk?"

"I don't know." Mac shook his head. "I've met this man, but I can't put a name to his face."

Though getting dressed was the last thing Mac wanted to do, he zipped his jeans and shoved his feet into his new boots. He turned toward Abby who was fastening the last buttons on her blouse. Her snug leather slacks outlined her slender hips. Even with clothes on, the woman was hot. Smoking hot.

Smoke. He sniffed the air.

Abby pivoted to face him. "Do you smell that?"

He stared at the closed door of the bedroom and saw a flicker of orange light at the edge. *Fire.* "Grab your stuff."

Gun in hand, he flung the bedroom door open. A blast of heat rolled over them. The front room of Aunt Lucille's cabin was in flames. The sofa. The curtains. Fire licked at the edge of the walls, but it hadn't spread. The path to the front door was open.

Mac glanced at the propane heater in the bedroom. There was another heater in the living room. If the fire hit the propane, there would be an explosion.

They had to move fast. He turned to Abby.

"This is crazy," Abby said. "If they wanted us dead, they could have walked into the bedroom and opened fire."

"They didn't want to take the chance we might be awake." Mac stepped back into the bedroom. "Whoever set this fire is probably waiting for us outside."

"How do we get past them?"

He'd spent a lot of time at his Aunt Lucille's cabin and knew the terrain. There was an escape. "Out the kitchen door and over the cliff."

"What?"

"Trust me," he said. "I know a way down."

"Jumping off a cliff? That's a brilliant plan."

The braided rag rug caught fire. Orange flames darted closer to the propane heater. They couldn't stay here. "Have you got a better idea?"

She shook her head. "Let's do it."

Mac clasped her hand in his, praying that he remembered the route down from the granite boulder. There was a ledge, then a sheer drop to the rocks below. Trusting his instincts, he darted through the flames and into the kitchen where the fire had not yet spread. He flung open the door.

Still holding Abby's hand, he raced across the boulder, and over the cliff. Together, they slid down the face of the rock. For an instant, he thought he'd misjudged the escape and they would plummet heedlessly for a hundred feet. Then his feet hit the packed earth of a ledge. Abby was still beside him.

They had to go single file. He released her hand. "Follow me."

The narrow path made a steep descent. His feet slipped, and he went down, catching himself before he took a header through open space.

Looking over his shoulder, he saw Abby clinging to the granite wall.

He struggled upright and kept going down, balancing precariously, moving fast. Still on the path, they slipped behind a boulder that provided cover.

"Are you okay?" she asked.

"Just swell."

From the rocks above, they heard a ferocious explosion. Aunt Lucille's cabin was history.

Mac peeked out. The fire from the cabin turned the dawn sky to a fierce orange. At the top of the cliff, he thought he saw someone looking down. But there had been no gunfire. Their reckless escape method had taken their assailants by surprise.

"Now what?" Abby asked.

"We keep going."

It wasn't an easy descent to the trees, but Mac remembered the route. He and his friends had used this cliff to hone their rock-climbing skills. The hard part would be the final drop of about twelve feet which was perfect for practicing the necessary balance and gripping techniques. He and Abby didn't have time for a technical climb.

Mac got down on his hands and knees. "I'll slide down here. Then you come. I'll catch you."

She nodded.

He flattened himself against the rough granite and lowered his legs over the edge. For a moment, he was dangling in space, then he slid. When he hit the ground, he rolled backward, slamming against jagged stones and hard earth. Every one of his injuries screamed with renewed pain.

But when he rose to his feet and took inventory, he found no broken bones, no sprains.

He looked back toward the flames from the cabin. Clearly silhouetted, he saw a figure in black, staring down. It was a woman.

She lifted her arm and checked her wristwatch.

He knew that gesture. Sheila! His partner was the dirty cop.

That was why she hadn't come into the cabin and shot them while they slept. Sheila was a coward. As he watched, she stepped back, running away.

"Come on, Abby."

Following his example, she lowered herself over the edge. As she slid, he caught her in his arms.

There would be time later to tell her about Sheila. Right now, they had to run.

THOUGH ABBY was in good physical condition, Mac had pushed her to the edge of her limits. It hadn't been too bad when they were running downhill, dodging through the trunks of lodgepole pines and other conifers. But they'd been headed uphill for the last mile, and she was miserable.

Her lungs ached. Her mouth was horribly dry. The muscles in her legs had gone from tense to slack to a state where she couldn't even feel the pain. She sank down on a fallen log. "Wait."

He halted and walked back toward her. Instead of looking at her, his gaze focused on the faraway cliffside where they'd almost been burned alive.

She peered back through the trees. A tall plume of smoke smudged the overcast morning sky, but she saw no sign of flames. "The fire department must have arrived in time to keep the blaze from spreading."

"A damn good thing. Though the cabin was separated from the trees, there's forest all around here. This could have been a major fire." He looked up. "It's going to rain soon. That'll help."

"I'm sorry about your aunt's cabin."

"It's a sign," he said. "I never should have thought I could come home again."

"Bitter?"

"Hell, yes. How long have I been here? Less than a week. I've gotten in a shoot-out on the streets of Vail. My friend Jess was nearly killed by somebody who was gunning for me. And Aunt Lucille's cabin is burned to the ground."

Unfortunately, all those things were true. Abby knew there was nothing she could say to make it better.

"It's time," he said, "for me to go back to the city where life is more calm."

"But this all started in Denver," she reminded him. "And none of it is your fault. Not Jess's injuries. Not your aunt's cabin. You can't blame yourself."

"Can't I?" A cool cynicism shaded his expression. "I feel like crap, Abby. Let's not start looking for silver linings."

"It hasn't been all bad." She massaged her thighs, hoping the circulation would come back. "After all, you met me."

"And that is a very good thing." He took her hand and pulled her to her feet. "We need to keep going. It's not much farther."

She groaned. "Where?"

"Yankee Lake. We can stop there and catch our breath."

"Is there a convenience store in Yankee Lake?" She plodded, putting one foot in front of the other with effort. "Because I'm really hungry."

"It's a regular town," he said. "A ghost town."

"Swell."

As far as she was concerned, this adventure was over. The fire at the cabin signaled an end to whatever plans Mac had for luring Dirk into a trap. They had no car. No weapon. And they were on the run.

Her cell phone was itching in her pocket, and she couldn't wait to call Julia at the safe house. Or Paul. Or anybody who would offer a hot meal and a ride back to civilization.

At the top of a rise, they came upon a small, nearly round lake in a secluded, pristine setting. Though the mirrorlike water probably wasn't completely safe to drink, Abby knelt on the rocky shore, cupped her hands and brought the cold, clear liquid to her mouth. Heavenly!

Mac did the same. He splashed the cold water on his face and ran a hand through his thick hair. His general appearance—after running through the forest for a couple of hours—was craggy and rugged in spite of the blue silk turtleneck and expensive leather jacket. Maybe he wasn't the pinnacle of boutique fashion, but he was gorgeous and manly to her. "When we were back at the cabin," she said, "you saved my life."

"Because you trusted me when I led you over the edge of a cliff. You took the leap."

A leap of faith. She drank again. After a few more gulps, she felt almost human. "Now it's time for you to trust me. There's no way we can put together a sting on Dirk."

He stood and strode toward the ruins of several log cabins. He leaned against a free-standing stone fireplace which was all that was left of a cabin that had disintegrated over time. His cell phone was in his hand, and she prayed he would speed dial his friend Paul, the deputy sheriff.

Abby struggled to her feet and went to stand beside him. Under cloudy skies, the tumbled-down walls of the deserted town seemed gray and insubstantial as a ghostly mirage. A dirt road ran through the center of six dismantled structures of log and stone. The mountains had almost reclaimed this land.

"I saw something back at the cabin," he said. "I caught a glimpse of somebody dressed in black."

"The same guy who chased us in Vail?"

"No."

Though he glanced away, she could read his expression and she knew he'd recognized the person who set the fire. "Who was it?"

"My partner, Sheila."

Abby was surprised. When she'd studied the dossier on Mac, information on his partner was part of the package. Though Sheila's behavior at the warehouse indicated a clumsiness in the execution of her duty, her record showed that she'd been promoted quickly. She must have shown some ability. "Are you sure?"

"I didn't see her face clearly, but she made a gesture." He lifted his arm as if to check his wristwatch. "That's a habit with her."

"Sheila is the dirty cop."

"When I look back, it makes sense," he said. "On the night of the warehouse shootout, we were headed to an investigation in north Denver. She insisted on making two stops. She slowed us down, timed it so we'd be the ones closest to the warehouse when the call came through."

"She set you up?"

He shook his head. "I don't think she's that smart. More likely, she was supposed to shoot Dante Williams before he gave away her identity. But I did it for her."

"But she wasn't the person who killed Leo in Vail," Abby said. "You said that was a man."

"Which means she's working with somebody else." He checked his cell phone. "There are two calls from her."

"She must have seen you at the cabin," Abby said. "Why didn't she follow us?"

"Climbing down a sheer rock face into a forest isn't Sheila's style." Not without a latte clutched in her fist. "Should I call her back?"

"Definitely not," Abby said. "She'll hear in your voice that you're onto her."

"You're right." He snapped his phone closed and put it in his pocket. "I'll take care of Sheila later. Right now, there's still Dirk to deal with."

Abby couldn't believe her ears. "You're not still thinking about a sting, are you?"

"I'm not giving up."

A surge of anger boosted her energy. She turned on her heel and walked away from him, marching down the center of the ghost town. A sting on Nicholas Dirk? Why couldn't Mac understand the futility of that plan? In addition to no backup, they were a weapon short and had no getaway car.

Still, she didn't argue with him. The time had come for deception. She hated lying to Mac, but there was simply no other choice. A plan sprang, fully formed, into her head. This kind of work—the art of deception— was what she did best.

When Mac stepped up beside her, she applied a bit of misdirection. "Tell me about this deserted town, Yankee Lake. Why would anybody want to live here?"

"For one thing, there's water." He gestured

toward the lake. "For another, there was a gold mine farther up that dirt road. They mined it dry and moved on."

"Just picked up and left everything behind?"

"Little mining towns like this one generally weren't family-oriented. There might be a saloon or a small brothel. All the men needed was a place to sleep and keep warm while they made their fortune in the mine."

The first step in Abby's plan was getting her hands on Mac's cell phone, which he'd tucked away in his jacket pocket. It was easy for her to glide her arms around him in a casual embrace. "Would you have liked living in the old west?"

"Doubtful." His arms closed around her. "I like modern conveniences too much. Good food. Fast cars. And soft beds."

"I'm with you." She slid her hand into his pocket, closed her fingers around his phone and extracted it. "I'm also fond of modern plumbing, but I'll have to improvise. Would you excuse me for a minute while I answer nature's call?"

"You surprise me, Abby."

"Because I need to pee?"

"Because you're not fighting me about doing a sting on Dirk."

"I know better than to argue with a determined man." She gave him a quick kiss and stepped away. "Be back in a minute."

As soon as she was out of Mac's sight, Abby speed dialed Paul. When he answered, she talked fast. "This is Abby. I'm with Mac. I need for you to come here. Alone. Can you do that?"

"Yes," he said firmly.

"I mean it. No other officers."

"He's my friend. I want to see him get out of this in one piece. Where are you?""

"Yankee Lake. And don't tell Mac I contacted you."

"On my way," Paul said. "I can be there within a half an hour."

As she disconnected the call, guilt washed over her. She was deceiving Mac, fulfilling his expectation that all women were sneaky and manipulative. *Too bad.* She argued with herself. *This was for his own damn good.*

The problem now was to keep Mac here until his friend arrived. On her way back to Yankee Lake, she dropped his cell phone near the chimney where he had checked for messages.

He was seated on the remains of a log wall, looking out at the lake. A light rain had begun to fall, causing circular ripples on the smooth surface. She sat beside him.

"I've been thinking," he said, "about the sting. It might be safest to lure Dirk to someplace public where we could make the supposed exchange for the disk."

"An exchange for what?" she asked.

"A hundred thousand?" He glanced toward her.

"Is that enough?"

"If you're asking for cash, it's too much. I doubt Dirk has that kind of money on hand. And cash is bulky." Though she didn't want to encourage his sting idea, Abby offered expert advice which she fervently hoped would be unnecessary. Paul would be here soon and would help her talk Mac out of this crazy scheme. "Tell Dirk that you'll want to make a money transfer to an off-shore account via computer. All he needs to bring with him is his laptop."

"That's good," Mac said. "I'll ask for five hundred thousand in exchange for the disk."

He reached toward his pocket for his cell phone. His hand came out empty. "Where's my phone?"

She gave him the most innocent look she could muster. "You had it earlier."

When he rose from the log and strode back to the fireplace stones, she followed. Her mind raced. She hadn't expected Mac to make the call so soon.

While he searched around in the dry grasses, she said, "We probably ought to work out all the details before you contact Dirk. These kinds of things take planning."

"What's to plan? I tell him to meet me and bring his computer."

"Listen, Mac. I've been in on sting operations before. Every detail has to be worked out. You need to know what you're after. Are you going to record Dirk's confession? What do we do if he shows up with half a dozen henchmen? How do we make a safe getaway?"

"Not a problem," Mac said. "The mere fact that Dirk would show up and be willing to part with big bucks ought to be enough for a search warrant."

"You don't know that. Not for sure."

He located his cell phone in the grass where she'd dropped it. As he picked it up, he eyed her suspiciously. "But I know somebody I can ask."

"Slow down." She struggled to keep her voice calm. "We don't need to figure this out in the next five minutes."

"I want this to be over." He hit the speed dial on his phone. "I'm calling my lieutenant back in Denver. Hal Perkins."

"You won't be able to reach him. It's Saturday."

"I have his cell number."

"Wait."

There must have been a note of desperation in her tone because Mac turned off the call. When he came toward her, she saw his intense determination. He was a strong man, a man with a straightforward goal, and she felt miserable for betraying him.

He brushed his knuckles across her cheek. "Try to understand, Abby."

"All I can see is that you're rushing toward disaster."

"I have to clear my name," he said. "I'm a good cop. That's my identity. That's who I am. If I lose my reputation, I'm nothing."

"Not to me."

"That's a load of bull." The light of his smile blinded her. "If I was a dirty cop, you'd have nothing to do with me."

"But you're not. I know that."

"After Dirk is put away, everybody else will know it, too." Again, he flipped open his cell phone. "We should start walking. It's only about a mile to a little general store, and I know the guy who runs it. I'm thinking I can use his car."

She couldn't allow him to leave Yankee Lake before Paul arrived. Abby needed another diversion.

She strode toward him and faked a misstep. When she hit the ground, she cried out. "My ankle."

Mac raced to her side and knelt beside her. "Are you okay?"

"It hurts." She forced fake tears to her eyes. "I think I sprained it."

"Let me take a look."

"Ow! Don't touch it."

He easily lifted her from the ground and carried her to a place where she could sit. She groaned loudly and trembled with fake pain.

After this performance, he might never trust her again. But she was doing the right thing. She had to believe that she was saving both their lives.

Chapter Sixteen

Her injury was a problem for Mac. He knelt beside Abby and gently probed her ankle. Though he felt no swelling or broken bones, every movement of her long, slender leg caused her to wince in genuine pain. Hiking was out of the question.

"I'll have to leave you here," he said. "I can hike out and arrange for transportation to get you to a hospital."

"Don't leave me, Mac. Please."

Though it was out of character for Abby to be so clingy, he could understand her reluctance to be left alone in a deserted ghost town at the end of a dirt road, helpless against attackers. The rain clouds overhead made the skies dismal and gray.

"I'll have to carry you," he said.

"I have a better idea," she said quickly.

"We could call Julia. Since we know that Sheila is the dirty cop, there's no reason to suspect anybody at the safe house."

Mac didn't want to refuse Abby anything, especially not when she was in pain. Still, he said, "No. Julia will want the feds to take over this sting. I need to do this myself."

"Why?"

"I want to see the look on Dirk's face when I tell him it's all over."

"Pure revenge." Her adorable forehead crinkled in a frown. "That's a dangerous motive."

"Maybe," Mac said. "But Dirk nearly killed my friend. He burned down my aunt's cabin."

"That was Sheila."

"Acting on instructions from Dirk."

Though he knew better than to indulge a need for revenge, he had to go after Dirk himself. In his years as a cop, Mac had seen too many criminals get off with a wink and a plea. They twisted the law until justice was nothing more than a faint memory. That wasn't going to happen. Not this time. Nicholas Dirk was going to prison.

"You're having doubts," Abby said. Her

brown eyes widened appealingly. "We need somebody else in law enforcement to help."

"I'll get a second opinion."

"Where from?"

"I'll make that call to Lieutenant Perkins."

Hal Perkins was surprised to hear from Mac. His first piece of advice echoed Abby's concerns. "You can't handle this sting alone. You need backup."

"There won't be a problem," Mac said. "I'll do it in a public place."

"You could be endangering private citizens."

Mac had already thought of that. "A crowded place."

"In Vail?" His gravelly voice rumbled.

"I was thinking of the Burger Barn. No way would Dirk open fire in a place like that."

There was silence on the other end of the line. Then Perkins said, "It might work."

"If Dirk shows, it's proof that he's willing to pay a huge amount of blackmail. Is that enough for a warrant?"

"Getting a search warrant isn't the problem. I'd strongly advise that—"

"Thanks, Lieutenant. See you in a few

days." Mac ended the call and returned to Abby's side. "Perkins thinks this could work."

"It's not safe," she said. "When the FBI plans a sting, it takes hours of coordination, planning and experience. You've never done this before."

The rumble of a vehicle coming down the road surprised Mac. He whipped around and saw Paul's Land Rover. How had his friend figured out where he was?

As Paul came to a stop, he climbed out of the car and stalked toward them, talking as he approached. "I ought to kick your butt, Mac Granger."

"Nice to see you, too. How's Jess?"

"He's doing a whole lot better than you are." He towered over Mac like an angry grizzly. "Aunt Lucille's cabin is burned to the ground. And it's damn lucky the flames didn't spread."

"How did you know where to find me?"

"I've been looking," Paul said. "Ever since last night. Did you really think you could walk away from a shoot-out on the streets of Vail village?"

Mac shrugged. "I didn't think anybody saw us. Except for the guy who was trying to kill us."

Paul took a step back. "Somebody tried to kill you?"

"The same guy who murdered Leo Fisher," Mac said. "He came after us. We had to run. So we went to Aunt Lucille's to catch a few hours sleep. That's when somebody set the cabin on fire, trying to kill us again."

Paul peered around his shoulder to where Abby was still sitting. "Is all this true?"

She nodded.

"I'm talking here," Mac said. "Look at me. Paul, you know I haven't done anything wrong."

Paul lumbered over to the log where Abby was sitting. He sank down beside her. "You've got to turn yourself in, Mac."

Why the hell was everybody—including Paul—so quick to draw the worst conclusion? "I'm only going to say this one more time. I haven't done anything wrong."

Paul exhaled a weary sigh. "The sheriff found a gun on the street in Vail. There hasn't been time for ballistics or an autopsy on the victim yet. But they have a bullet. And it's the right caliber for the gun. We're assuming this is the weapon used to kill Leo Fisher."

Mac nodded, unsure where Paul was going with this information. "Finding the murder weapon is a good thing."

"Not this time," Paul said. "It's your gun, Mac. The serial number matches your service Glock."

Though Mac held himself in tight control, he felt the blood drain from his face. The web of suspicion around him drew tighter. "I turned in my gun and badge for the duration of the I.A. investigation. It can't be mine."

"I'm just giving you the facts."

And the evidence, the damning evidence. He'd been framed. "I don't suppose there were any prints on the gun."

"A partial. It belongs to a Denver cop named Jeremiah Wallace. Do you know him?"

"The name is familiar, but I can't place it. Jeremiah Wallace? Jerry Wallace?"

His brain scrolled through the personnel at the Denver P.D. Beat cops. Vice cops. Detectives. Sergeants. Lieutenants. Who was Jeremiah Wallace? With a satisfying click, he remembered. Jerry Wallace was about six feet tall, brown hair and eyes. He was a smoker. A ladies' man. Not as good-looking as he thought he was.

Mac remembered his face. Jerry Wallace was the guy he'd spotted outside Dirk's party, the guy who had followed Leo and Vince Elliot. And there was another connection. "He dated Sheila."

"Were they lovers?" Abby asked.

"Probably. Sheila gets around. Half the time we're on duty, she's blabbing about the details of her love life. I try not to listen."

"This is her doing," Abby said firmly. She turned to Paul to explain, "Mac spotted his partner, Sheila, at the cabin fire. She's the dirty cop. She must have gotten hold of the gun back in Denver. This guy, Jerry Wallace, must have been the shooter."

"Whatever the explanation, it doesn't look good," Paul said. "The best thing for you to do, Mac, is turn yourself in and let us sort out what happened."

That advice was exactly what Mac would have said to someone in his situation: Step back and let the police proceed with their investigation. But he didn't know who he could trust, didn't know how far this conspiracy reached. The Eagle County Sheriff's department could be involved through Dirk.

He had only one chance to nab Dirk. As

soon as Mac turned himself in, it would be common knowledge that the disk had been destroyed in the shoot-out. He'd have no leverage. He hated to trade on his friendship with Paul, but there was no other way. "I've got to ask you a question. Do you believe I killed Leo Fisher?"

"Hell, no."

"Do you think I'm taking bribes?"

Paul rose slowly from the log. He squared his shoulders as though taking a physical stand. "You're the most honest man I've ever known. And one of the smartest. When you became a homicide detective, I was proud. You, me and Jess. We all turned out pretty damn good."

"We did."

"All I want is the truth," Paul said. "I want to know what son of a bitch is responsible for shooting Jess. If that means disregarding my duty as a deputy sheriff, so be it."

"Will you help me?"

Paul removed his badge and slipped it into his pocket. "What do you need?"

"Three hours time. And the use of a vehicle."

"You got it, Mac. Don't let me down."

CRUISING THROUGH the condo-lined streets near Vail village in Paul's Rover, Abby's mind raced. She glared through the windshield from the passenger seat. Every instinct she'd honed as an undercover agent told her Mac's plan to trap Nicholas Dirk was a mistake, but there was no way to convince him to call off this sting.

He'd already made the phone call to Dirk. The time for their meeting was set. One hour from now. This was crazy!

"You're quiet," Paul said.

"Because I'm gritting my teeth." Her scheme to get Paul involved had certainly backfired. Not only had he refused to take Mac into protective custody, but the burly deputy was aiding Mac's sting. He'd even arranged for them to use Jess's Jeep.

He frowned. "You don't approve of Mac's plan."

"No."

"We've got to let him do it. It's important for him to clear his good name."

She glanced over her shoulder into the rear of Paul's Rover and studied Mac—this incredibly stubborn man who was determined to plunge head-long into disaster. In contrast to her rising panic, he was cool. His blue eyes shone with the firm conviction that he was doing the right thing.

She couldn't fault him for lack of bravery—the same sort of blind courage that inspired warriors to charge across an open field. Mac was ready to lay down his life in the pursuit of justice. Without a single thought for his own safety, he would take on a high-powered drug lord and all his henchmen. His annoying strength of character was evident in the set of his jaw and the steady calm that surrounded him. An admirable man. A handsome man.

He returned her gaze, and her careless heart fluttered. Sensory memories of their intimacy flooded her consciousness. Damn it! She knew better.

"We're here," Paul announced as he parked outside Jess's condo in Vail. "I wish you'd let me come with you for backup."

"Not necessary," Mac said. "Have you got the keys for Jess's Jeep?"

"We always keep spares for each other." Though Paul detached a small ring with a house key and car key from his larger key chain, he didn't hand it over. "At least, tell me where you're going to meet Dirk."

Mac rested a hand on his friend's shoulder. "If this goes wrong, I don't want to destroy your career along with my own. After I have the evidence on Dirk, I'll call you."

Paul turned over the keys. "Good luck."

Abby forced herself to remember her fake limp as she followed Mac to Jess's Jeep and climbed into the passenger seat. When Paul drove away, Mac started up the engine of the Jeep, then turned to her.

His voice was low and angry. "You lied to me, Abby."

Without flinching, she faced him. "I beg your pardon?"

"I don't know how you did it, but you called Paul. Then, you faked an ankle injury so I'd have to stay with you until he arrived."

Her lips pinched together. The worst thing to do when confronted with your own deception was to deny it or to make excuses.

"I wanted to trust you," he said. "I wanted to believe that you'd be different with me. But you can't stop the lies. It's who you are."

This was too unfair; she couldn't keep from responding. "I did it for your own good,

Mac. Going forward with this sting is fool-hardy and dangerous."

"Which is why I don't want you with me," he said. "But I can't leave you behind. As soon as you're by yourself, you'll call Julia and the feds will move in."

He was right, of course. "Good guess."

"I could tie you up and gag you," he said. "That way I could keep you safely out of the picture until this is over."

"You could try." Her own anger ignited. "But you won't. An attempt to tie me up would be incredibly stupid. Not only am I far from helpless, but you need me at your sting. If you go in alone, there's no reason why Dirk shouldn't blow you away."

As he considered her words, his eyes narrowed. "I hate that you lied to me."

"Then we're even," she said. "I hate that you're risking your life for something as stupid as revenge."

"It's more than that, Abby. This is about honor and truth and protecting the people I care about."

The anger that passed between them gen-erated its own heat, but the sensation was nothing like the warmth of their shared passion. This fire consumed her sense of joy and pleasure, leaving her aching and empty.

"What about me?" she asked. "Do you care about me?"

"God help me, I do."

Resentment tinged his voice, and she knew that he didn't want to care about her. Their nascent relationship was over. After her lie, he would never be able to fully trust her.

"Damn you, Mac Granger. I hate the way I feel about you. I hate that you're a good and honest man. I hate that when I look into your eyes, I'd follow you to hell and beyond."

"Is that so?"

"It is." She ripped her gaze away from his face. Later, there would be time to remember the joy she'd felt in his arms, the laughter they'd shared at Oktoberfest, the moments at Dirk's party when she'd turned to him for comfort. Right now, there was only one thing. Commitment. "I'll stick by you, Mac. Tell me the plan."

He pulled away from the curb. "I'll wait for Dirk at a booth inside Burger Barn. He already agreed to ransom the disk with a money transfer from his computer, but I want him to admit two things while I'm recording our conversation. First, that he was responsible for shooting Jess. Second, that he's been bribing Denver cops."

"And how do you intend to lead him toward these confessions?"

"I'm pretty good at interrogation when it doesn't involve a phony cover story. I'll manage."

"Assume that you do," she said. "Then what happens? After he spills his guts, how do you get out of Burger Barn alive?"

"I guess I'll have to give him the disk."

"The shattered disk?" she asked archly. "Keep in mind that he'll have his computer with him. You can't hand over a dummy."

"I'll tell him the truth," Mac said.

"Brilliant idea," she said sarcastically. "I'm sure a psychotic drug lord will respond to the truth."

His jaw tightened. "Have you got a better idea?"

"Actually, I do." In spite of her misgivings, she'd given the logistics of the sting some thought. "Let me take the meeting with Dirk."

"No way."

"Be sensible, Mac. This is my area of expertise. I've participated in sting operations before. I know how this works. After I have Dirk's confession, I'll identify myself as FBI and take him into custody. At that point, we contact Julia, and it's over."

"You call in backup," he said.

"That's right."

"And what do I do?"

"You wait outside Burger Barn. If Dirk tries to run, you're ready to follow."

For several minutes, he drove in silence. Then he said, "You're asking me to trust you."

"That's right."

"In spite of the fact that you've lied to me from the minute we met. False identities. Constant deceptions. In spite of the fact that you lied to me less than an hour ago."

"You know the truth about me," she said. "And you also know this. I'm not going to let you die."

"Compromise," he said. "I'll meet Dirk inside Burger Barn. And I'll arrest him. As soon as he shows, you call Julia and the feds can move in."

Chapter Seventeen

Inside Burger Barn, Mac chose a booth at the front window where he could look out into the parking lot and see Abby sitting behind the wheel of the Jeep. Her pale blond hair shimmered in the stray bits of sunlight that had begun to cut through the rain. If he could see her dark eyes, he knew they'd be poised and alert. She was a good cop, good at her job.

He hated that she'd lied to him. But what had he expected? Her livelihood was based on her talent for deception. She was trained in the arts of misdirection and betrayal. From the very start, he'd known he could never trust her.

And yet, she was here, taking part in his sting. In spite of the detriment to her FBI career, she was willing to follow him into hell and beyond. Those were her words. Into hell and beyond. Mac wasn't sure what to make of that statement, but it sounded a lot like loyalty to him.

After placing an order for a burger and fries, he glanced up at the clock above the front doorway. In less than ten minutes, Nicholas Dirk would walk through the door, and Mac would have the answers he wanted. He would know, without a shadow of a doubt, that Dirk was behind all the miserable things that had happened.

Instead, Mac recognized a very different person who strolled into Burger Barn. A heavyset man with a rolling gait. It was his lieutenant at the Denver P.D. Hal Perkins.

For a moment, Mac tried to convince himself that Hal was here to help. When they'd talked on the phone, Mac had mentioned setting his sting operation at the Burger Barn. But that conversation took place less than two hours ago. If Hal had been in Denver, he wouldn't have had time to get here. Which led to the obvious conclusion: Hal Perkins was already in Vail. As was Sheila. They were working together. They and the assassin— Jerry Wallace—were the dirty cops.

When Hal slid into the booth opposite him, Mac said, "I should have known that Sheila wasn't smart enough to handle this operation on her own."

"She's a cute little package," Hal rumbled in his deep voice, "but not a genius."

"My gun," Mac said. "You're the one who took my gun from where it was impounded and gave it to Jerry Wallace."

Hal's shaggy eyebrows lifted. "You already know about the gun, huh? And about Jerry?"

"That's right." He saw exhaustion etched deeply in the lines of Hal's jowly face. "Jerry was the assassin. He killed Leo Fisher and tried to kill me."

"A logical conclusion," Hal said.

"But it was Sheila who started the fire at my aunt's cabin. How did you track us down?"

"MacCloud was your mother's maiden name. And your aunt's name, too. It wasn't a stretch to locate her cabin where your car was parked." His heavy shoulders shrugged. "We're good at figuring these things out. We're cops."

"Dirty cops. Working for Nicholas Dirk."

"Funny thing," Hal said. "I've never actually met the man face to face."

"You just took his money. Handed off from one petty drug dealer to the next until the cash found its way into your pockets. I hope he paid you well enough to flee the country because you're not going to get away with this."

"I'm sure as hell going to try." He leaned across the tabletop. "Turn over the computer disk, Mac."

"I've got one question first."

"All you get is one."

Mac's former respect for this man had turned to disgust and hatred. It was all he could do to keep himself from reaching across the table and ripping into Hal's fat throat. "Who shot Jess?"

"That was a mistake."

"My friend almost died from that mistake."

Hal pointed a blunt fingertip. "Jerry was gunning for you."

"Acting on orders from Dirk?"

"I said you only got one question, Mac. But I'll give you this answer. Killing you was our idea. Sheila, Jerry and I knew that you were too good a cop. You'd eventually figure everything out. And we'd pay the price."

"So you decided to murder me."

"It was nothing personal. Hey, I always liked you, Mac. You're a hard worker and smart. The only problem is that you're too damned honest for your own good." He held out his hand. "The disk."

"Why the hell should I give it to you?" Mac glanced around the Burger Barn. Several patrons chatted comfortably at their tables, unaware of the life and death drama playing out at the window booth. "There are too many witnesses here. There's nothing you can do to me without getting caught."

Hal turned to the window and nodded toward the outside.

Mac followed his gaze. When he saw Sheila sitting in the passenger seat beside Abby, his anger took on a razor-sharp edge of fear. Abby was here because of him. She'd followed him into hell, and now her life was in danger.

"Let her go," Mac said. "You admitted that you made a mistake when you shot Jess. Don't make another by hurting her."

"Here's the plan," Hal said. "You do what I say or your girlfriend takes a bullet to the gut."

"Whatever you say." There was no choice. Mac could only bargain for time. Silently, he apologized to Abby. If they'd done things her way, they wouldn't be in this situation. If she hadn't been loyal to him, she'd be safe.

He could only hope there would be some way out. "What do you want me to do?"

"First, you give me the disk. Then you and I are going outside together. You'll drive my car. Your girlfriend will follow. That's all you need to know for now."

Mac reached into his pocket and retrieved the bloody envelope. He tossed it on the table. "You're welcome to it. One of Jerry's bullets shattered the disk."

"Son of a bitch." Hal barked a harsh laugh.

"All this," Mac said, "for a busted piece of plastic."

Hal slid out of the booth, took a ten from his wallet and threw it on the table. "Let's go, Mac."

ABBY SAT in the driver's seat of the Jeep with both hands on the wheel as instructed. The barrel of Sheila's gun poked into her ribs, but Abby wasn't the least bit afraid. In her mind, she'd already planned the moves she would make to disarm Sheila, who was too dumb to even be nervous.

All Abby had to do was wait for the right moment. She wished that she'd put through a call to the safe house, wished that she'd already contacted Julia Last and informed her that they needed backup. But Abby still hadn't seen Nicholas Dirk.

Sheila leaned toward her. "What's Mac like in bed?"

"Why do you care?"

"Just curious. I always thought he'd be hot, but he made it real clear that he didn't want a personal relationship with me. Something about being partners."

"Or he didn't find you attractive," Abby said archly. "Some men don't like stupid women."

"You've got no room to talk. You're the one with a gun in your belly."

Abby couldn't wait to kick Sheila's butt. She was extraordinarily annoying. "How much did you get paid in bribes?"

"A lot."

After a disdainful once-over, Abby said, "And you still dress like that? I guess it's true. You can't buy good taste."

"As if you'd know," Sheila said. "What's your story, anyway? Are you a protected witness?"

"I'm a fed," Abby said. "You understand what that means, don't you? If you kill me, the full wrath of the FBI will come down on your head. They have eyes everywhere. You'll never escape."

There was a flicker of panic in Sheila's eyes. Now would have been an excellent time to disarm her, but Dirk still hadn't shown up. And Abby didn't know what was happening with Mac.

Then she spotted him. He left the Burger Barn in the company of a heavyset man. "Who's that?"

"Hal Perkins," Sheila said. "He's our lieutenant, and he's working with me."

"What's he doing?"

"He's getting into the car with Mac. They're going to drive, and you're going to follow. Got it?"

Every fear Abby had about this sting had come to pass. She and Mac were captured without backup. They were going to be taken to some remote location where they'd be killed and their bodies hidden. And Nicholas

Dirk hadn't shown up. They wouldn't even have evidence to use against him.

It was small comfort that she'd been right in her assessment.

"Start the car," Sheila ordered.

No way would Abby drive to another location. The time for action was now. Right now. As she leaned forward to reach the dangling car keys, she lashed out with a karate chop to Sheila's nose. With the other hand, she shoved the barrel of the gun up and away from her body.

In reflex, Sheila pulled the trigger. The bullet shattered the windshield.

Abby yanked the car door open and leaped out. The sight that confronted her stopped her dead in her tracks. The heavyset man—Hal Perkins—held his gun to Mac's head.

For one instant, her gaze met Mac's. He winked.

In a sudden movement, he ducked and drove his elbow into his lieutenant's gut. The big man was no match for Mac, who followed his first jab with a second. He had the lieutenant's gun, and Hal Perkins lay on the ground unconscious.

"Not so fast," Sheila snarled.

Abby turned and saw the gun pointed directly at her.

Blood spurted from Sheila's nose, but her gaze was steady and desperate. She ordered, "Get back in the car. I need a hostage."

"Not me."

"Get in here now! Before I shoot you in the leg."

Though the gun trembled in her hand, Sheila wouldn't miss from this distance. Her hand extended outside the Jeep.

Abby was less than five feet away. If she rushed at Sheila, she would surely be hit.

She glanced toward Mac, who was trying to angle around and get a clear shot at Sheila. Again, this was a matter of timing. Abby didn't know how many seconds were left before Sheila pulled the trigger. How long would it take for Mac to get into position?

Abby heard the whine of a bullet. She saw the spark as it hit Sheila's gun. With a scream, Sheila dropped her weapon. Abby wasted no time in grabbing the gun.

But who had fired that bullet? It wasn't Mac. He hadn't been in the right position. He rushed toward her.

His hands grasped her upper arms. His

frantic eyes searched her face. "Are you all right? Are you hurt?"

"I'm fine."

He yanked her close against him. "I'll never doubt you again, Abby. Not ever."

Her heart soared. "You trust me?"

"With my life."

"Hey, you two. Break it up." Vince Elliot sauntered toward them, gun in hand. There were two uniformed Vail police officers with him. A few paces behind them was Nicholas Dirk.

"What the hell is going on?" Mac murmured.

"No worries," Vince said. "We're on the same side."

Mac nodded toward Dirk. "But you're with him."

"That's right. I've been working with Dirk for months. He's undercover."

While the Vail policemen took Hal Perkins and a sobbing Sheila Hartman into custody, Vince explained, "As you both know, we don't usually work with civilians. But Dirk has been involved in drug investigations before. He hires a lot of former addicts. One such employee relapsed, and

Dirk busted him. That's how he got involved."

Abby remembered the story Dirk had told her about the deterioration and death of his narcotics addicted mother and his sister. He'd told Abby that he participated in rehab efforts, including hiring programs.

"What about the bribes?" she asked.

"Somebody was paying off Sheila and her pals before vice got wind of their scheme," Vince said. "I suspect it was nickel-and-dime stuff. Protection money. And it went through several hands before it got to the dirty cops. We upped the ante, pretending the payoff was coming from Dirk and that he was some kind of drug lord."

"But he's not." She studied the face of the man she and Mac had suspected. His expression was relaxed. His amber-tinted eyes were friendly.

"I apologize for my rude behavior," Dirk said. "When you were at my house, I thought Mac was the dirty cop."

"So did I," Vince said. "It looked real bad for you, Mac. When you shot Dante Williams, he was about to give us the names of the dirty cops."

"What about Leo?" Abby asked.

"I tried to explain to him after Dirk's party," Vince said. "But he wouldn't listen. He was determined to get the bust."

And that blind determination killed him.

Mac gave her a final squeeze and stepped away from her. He extended his hand to Nicholas Dirk. "I misjudged you."

Dirk nodded as he shook hands. "And you wrecked my bulldozer."

"It made a hell of a weapon."

"The insurance will take care of it. I think my policy covers bulldozer combat."

Mac turned to Vince, and they also shook hands. Only moments ago, these men had been mortal enemies. Now they were on the same side.

Abby asked Vince, "How do you know that Mac's not dirty? That he's not working with his partner and his lieutenant?"

"When Mac called Dirk to sell the disk and said they'd meet at Burger Barn, I got here first," Vince said. "The woman who waited on Mac is a cop. She put a bug on the table. We heard the entire conversation with Hal Perkins."

"Which reminds me," Mac said. "I've still

got a burger waiting inside. Abby, can I buy you lunch?"

"That's the least you can do."

Inside the Burger Barn, Mac and Abby got a standing ovation from the patrons who had watched the whole dramatic scene from the front window.

One of Mac's old buddies from high school patted him on the back. "Good to have you back. Things were getting a little dull around here."

"I'm not back to stay." He glanced at Abby. "At least, not yet."

After they were served burgers and a mountain of fries on the house, he looked across the table at her. "You saved my life."

"Twice," she said. "Does three times make me a lady?"

"You already are a lady." He glanced down at his heaping plate of Burger Barn's finest cuisine. "I appreciate that you aren't gloating about my attempted sting."

"It all turned out okay," she said. "Next time, maybe you'll listen to me."

"Next time?"

She picked up her burger. "Don't even

think you're getting rid of me, Mac. Not after what we've been through."

"Getting rid of you is the last thing on my mind."

"And the first is food."

She bit into her burger, and he did the same. They hadn't eaten since last night at Dirk's party.

For a while, they simply ate the juicy hamburgers and crisp, hot fries drenched in ketchup. He couldn't help watching her, noticing the way she'd take a bite and then dab at the corner of her mouth. She tossed her head, and her platinum hair shimmered.

"What's the real color of your hair?" he asked.

"It's been ages since I've gone natural, but it used to be a kind of reddish brown."

"I want to see it that way." He reached across the table and clasped her hand. "I want to be with you, Abby. All the time."

Before Abby could answer, another person joined them at their table. Julia Last said, "It's quite an adventure you've both had."

He was glad to report to Julia that everything was resolved, the bad guys were in custody and it had not been necessary to mention that her lodge was actually run by the FBI.

"But I do have a question," Abby said. "Why was Roger Flannery following us in Vail?"

"I sent him," Julia said. "I thought it would be good experience for him, and it wouldn't hurt if you had backup. Unfortunately, he lost you before anything happened. It was sheer dumb luck that he happened to spot you when you came here. Then he called me."

"So you were outside? Watching the whole thing?"

She nodded. "I guess Roger and I were backup for your backup."

"Amazing," Mac said. At the moment when he'd been sitting at the booth with Hal Perkins and feeling completely alone, he had two sets of cops watching his back. "I guess we were never in danger, after all."

"Not unless you count the cabin fire, the explosion and the shoot-out in Vail," Abby said.

Julia rose to her feet. "Are you coming back to the lodge?"

"I don't think so," Mac said. "There are places I want to take this lady. Starting with the white water on the Roaring Fork River."

Slowly, Abby nodded, granting consent. Her smile was the most beautiful sight he'd ever seen. "Then you'll show me the sunrise on the Sangre de Christos."

"And I'll teach you to ski."

Julia rapped her knuckles on the tabletop. "Sounds like a long trip to me. And a happy one."

Mac couldn't remember a time when he'd been so happy. Abby would come with him. They'd travel, and he'd learn all about her. Every day would be a brand-new adventure.

* * * * *

*Be sure to read Cassie Miles's
next Harlequin Intrigue,
MURDER ON THE MOUNTAIN,
available April 2006.*

HARLEQUIN®
INTRIGUE®

WE'LL LEAVE YOU BREATHLESS!

If you've been looking for thrilling tales of contemporary passion and sensuous love stories with taut, edge-of-the-seat suspense—then you'll love Harlequin Intrigue!

Every month, you'll meet six new heroes who are guaranteed to make your spine tingle and your pulse pound. With them you'll enter into the exciting world of Harlequin Intrigue— where your life is on the line and so is your heart!

THAT'S INTRIGUE—
ROMANTIC SUSPENSE
AT ITS BEST!

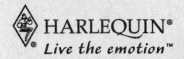

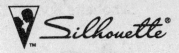

HARLEQUIN®
Presents

**The world's bestselling romance series...
The series that brings you your favorite authors,
month after month:**

Helen Bianchin...Emma Darcy
Lynne Graham...Penny Jordan
Miranda Lee...Sandra Marton
Anne Mather...Carole Mortimer
Susan Napier...Michelle Reid

and many more uniquely talented authors!

Wealthy, powerful, gorgeous men...
Women who have feelings just like your own...
The stories you love, set in exotic, glamorous locations...

HARLEQUIN®
Presents

Seduction and Passion Guaranteed!

HPDIR104

![Harlequin Historicals logo] **Harlequin Historicals®**
Historical Romantic Adventure!

*From rugged lawmen and
valiant knights to defiant heiresses
and spirited frontierswomen,
Harlequin Historicals will
capture your imagination with
their dramatic scope, passion
and adventure.*

*Harlequin Historicals . . .
they're too good to miss!*

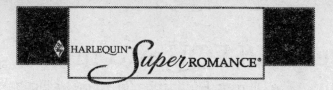

HARLEQUIN® *Super*ROMANCE®

...there's more to the story!

Superromance.
A *big* satisfying read about unforgettable
characters. Each month we offer *six* very different
stories that range from family drama to adventure
and mystery, from highly emotional stories to
romantic comedies—and much more! Stories
about people you'll believe in and care about.
Stories too compelling to put down....

Our authors are among today's *best* romance
writers. You'll find familiar names and talented
newcomers. Many of them are award winners—
and you'll see why!

If you want the biggest and best
in romance fiction, you'll get it
from Superromance!

Emotional, Exciting, Unexpected...

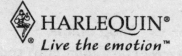

HARLEQUIN®
® *Live the emotion*™